MY WIFE'S SECRETS

WENDY OWENS

ORANGEWILLOW PUBLISHING

Cover Design: The Cover Collection

Developmental Editing: A Book A Day Editing

Copy Editing: Editing 4 Indies

Proofing: Karen Lawson

Proofing: Twin Tweaks Editing

Formatting: Wendy Owens

https://wendyowensbooks.com/

ALSO BY WENDY OWENS

DON'T MISS THE NEXT PSYCHOLOGICAL THRILLER BY WENDY OWENS

Do you want to make sure you don't miss any upcoming releases or giveaways? Be sure to sign up for my newsletter at http://signup.wendyowensbooks.com/

DEDICATION

For my readers, thanks for sticking with me.

1

My wife is being released from prison today. Correction, my ex-wife is being released today. I'm not sure how I feel about it. I know how I should feel. I'm married to someone else now, and we have a child. I know in my heart I shouldn't feel anything about today, but I can't seem to stop myself from being haunted by the life I had before this one.

Sometimes, there are moments when I forget the past few years, and I'll get excited that it's time to head home to Lizzy. The memories linger in my mind, and it feels like only yesterday when I would walk in the door and find her standing there to greet me. It wasn't yesterday, though. It might as well have been a lifetime ago. Even though Lizzy is being released, it doesn't change anything. My choices in the past wrecked so many lives, including my own. I can't do that again. I won't. My daughter deserves more than that.

"Nathan." Evelyn's voice breaks through my thoughts. "What are we going to do about Liz?"

My chest constricts when she says her name. I don't like the way it sounds when it leaves her lips. Maybe it's because it reminds me of the night Evelyn confessed to me that she visited my ex-wife in prison. Evelyn was worried I was angry with her, as though it was a betrayal for her to go see Liz. I couldn't tell her it wasn't anger I'd felt. It was sadness. I was sad that Evelyn saw Lizzy in prison before I did. I tried for so long to work up the courage to go, but I never did.

I clear my throat. "What do you mean what are we going to do?" When the words leave my lips, I can hear how annoyed I sound.

How could I have let things get so out of control? I could have asked myself this same question multiple times in the past few years. I loved being married to Lizzy. I'm not a hopeless romantic, but I would say she was my soul mate if anyone ever asked. I knew it from the moment I saw her at a frat party and watched at least half a dozen guys strike out with her that night. Initially, I saw her as a challenge—a mountain for me to climb. Within the first five minutes of talking to her, though, I knew she was special.

Lizzy was nothing like the rich, spoiled girls I usually dated. She wasn't impressed by the car people drove or their clothes. I doubt she could have picked a designer label out of a lineup when I met her. Books were the key to her soul. She devoured as many books as she could get her hands on and would much rather spend her time talking to people about the world she discovered on those pages. I loved her curiosity. It was also the first thing that faded from her after we lost our son.

It's easy to look back now and see all the mistakes I made, but at the time, all I could feel was pain. I was hurting, and I was too concerned with my pain to consider Lizzy was pulling away not because she no longer loved me but because she was also lost in the despair of losing a child. That crack in our relationship was the perfect opportunity for someone like Alison to enter our lives. She was my assistant at work. It was cliché, and I had always told myself I was better than that, given what I had witnessed with my own father. I wasn't.

I remember the day it started. I fought with Lizzy that morning. She used to get up with me in the morning and have breakfast with me, but in recent months, she often remained in bed until the afternoon. I tried. I made her breakfast and brought it to our room. When I woke her, she told me she wasn't hungry. I insisted she at least eat something. We went back and forth. I pushed, probably too hard, but I wanted my wife back. She threw the tray, screaming at me to leave her alone. I was so mad. I can still remember how hot the skin on my face was when I was driving to work.

Alison immediately sensed I was in a terrible mood and suggested we go to lunch and get my mind off whatever seemed to have me so worked up. The voice in the back of my head told me it was a bad idea, but I ignored it. When she leaned in and kissed me that first time, I didn't push her away. Things got out of control before I could get a handle on them. I told myself it was just the one time, but I liked the way Alison made me feel. She needed me to take care of her. I wanted to take care of Lizzy, but she wanted nothing to do with me. I tried to end things with Alison so many times, but I lost more control of the situation every time I did. By the end, I was paying for the house Alison was living in, and she told me she was pregnant.

My relationship with Evelyn felt similar to how things with Alison started. Lizzy went to prison for the murder of my mistress, Alison. I was conflicted by all the feelings I had at the time. I felt betrayed and disgusted after finding out she had been stalking Alison, but I also missed her. What kind of man misses a woman who could do something like that? That was when I met Evelyn. She was the friend I needed. I never intended for anything more with her, yet here I am, married to this woman I barely know anything about and raising a child with her.

"What do I mean?" she repeats, and I can tell she's surprised by my reaction. "Do you think she'll leave us alone now that she's managed to manipulate her way out of her sentence?"

I hesitate, unsure how to react to Ev's question. My mind focuses on the word manipulate. The truth is, I can see now that Lizzy didn't manipulate anyone. Evelyn didn't want me anywhere near the retrial, but there was so much press around the case I was able to stay up to date on it even though I wasn't in the courtroom. Evelyn thought my presence at court would only embolden Lizzy and cause her to think I wanted her back in my life, though sometimes I wonder if it was because she was more worried I would want Lizzy back.

Lizzy's lawyer presented a compelling case. During Lizzy's first trial, evidence gathered at the crime scene had not been fully processed. A key piece was DNA on the murder weapon that did not belong to Lizzy or the victim. Lizzy's new lawyer discovered the report that should have been attached to the evidence disclosures was missing, and it was unclear if the evidence was ever fully processed. After that was revealed, the DNA was run through a database. It came back that it belonged to a woman named Patty Dane.

Evelyn had every reason to worry. I was questioning if I had made a mistake. Lizzy never denied planning the murder, so it was easier to believe it had been her, but then I wasn't so sure. The court decided that evidence was enough to free Lizzy, and I kept finding myself thinking about how I had let the woman I loved down a second time.

I shake my head. "I don't think we have to worry about Liz," I reply, avoiding my wife's gaze. It isn't as if any of this matters anymore. Even if I wanted Lizzy back, she wouldn't take me. A man can only betray you so many times before you hate him. Besides that, I'm a dad now. I won't be like my father. I will be a part of my kid's life.

"And if you're wrong?" she asks me pointedly.

I close my eyes and lean back in my chair, shaking my head. "Then I'll take care of it." I try not to think about my life before Evelyn. About my life when Lizzy and I were happy. A life I wish I realized at the time was pretty close to perfect. Sure, we had problems, but if I could do things over again, I would. I now know how much worse things can get.

"What does that even mean?" Ev's voice cracks, revealing the fear behind her words. Sometimes, I feel bad for her. I can't imagine what it must be like. I think she knows I still love Lizzy. I don't mean to, but I don't think it's something I can stop.

I appreciate Ev because I was in such a dark place when she showed up. I met her at a grief counseling session. We started talking after the meeting, and I connected with her, though it was nothing romantic. She was there whenever I needed someone to listen. She was newer to town and didn't have a lot of friends, so we filled a void for each other. It never crossed my mind that we would start a relationship that was more than friends. I don't even remember how it happened, but I woke up in bed with her. I didn't think I had been that drunk, but clearly, I was wrong. Evelyn got the wrong idea. She assumed the night meant more than it had. I told myself I would do the right thing and tell her I was no good for her and she should find a man who could care about her the way she deserved. That was when Ev told me she was pregnant.

I reach out and grip my wife's wrists, pulling her onto my lap. She wraps her arms around my neck and heaves a breath before I hear it catch in her throat as she trembles slightly. I swallow and do my best to comfort her, trying not to betray that I'm worried about how I'll handle things if Lizzy shows up on our doorstep.

"The restraining order sends a very clear message to Lizzy," I state. That had been Evelyn's idea. I didn't think it was necessary, but it seemed to give her peace of mind, so I went along with it. "You and Madison are my family now. Quit worrying." I avoided Lizzy at all costs because I wasn't sure how seeing her would affect me. This time, I need to be a better man, for Madison.

"You don't understand," Ev says as a tear escapes.

"What don't I understand?" I press.

"I haven't told you everything," she confesses, and I feel my stomach start to twist. I hate secrets. "I knew you'd be angry with her if I told you."

"Angry with whom?"

Ev breaks down into heavy sobbing.

I place my fingers under her chin and force her eyes to meet mine. "Tell me," I urge.

She takes a moment to regain her composure and clears her throat. "The day that Liz signed the divorce papers, she said . . . something . . ."

"What did she say?"

Ev shakes her head, the hesitation taking hold. "I can't."

"I can't keep us safe if I don't know everything," I remind her.

She pulls her chin from my grasp, refusing to look at me.

"I won't be upset. I promise," I say.

She takes a deep breath and looks back at me. "I know I should have told you when it happened, but I was so worried about what you would do if you knew. When I was leaving that day, I made a terrible mistake. I thought maybe Liz would be happy to know that you were finally going to be a dad."

"Oh, Ev," I say with a heavy breath. I can only imagine how painful it was for Lizzy to receive that news.

Evelyn wipes her cheeks with her sleeve. "She was so

mad. She told me she was going to get out of there, and when she did, she was coming for her family."

"What?" I gasp, surprised by the revelation. "Why would you have told her that?"

Evelyn pushes off me and stands, crossing her arms. "Are you blaming me?"

I am. "No, of course not. It's just, you didn't think maybe that was something you shouldn't have shared with her?"

"If she loved you as much as she claimed to, I thought she would be happy for you." I rolled my eyes at her reasoning.

"Why didn't you tell me what she said?"

"I should have. I thought she was just venting. I never thought Liz would actually get out of prison. I'm so scared, Nathan," Ev yelps before she buries her head into her hands, breaking down again into incoherent whimpers.

I stand and put my arms around her. "Come on, you don't need to cry."

"You hate me, don't you?"

"Don't be silly." I sigh. "You need to stop worrying. I'm not going to let anyone hurt you," I proclaim, remembering a similar promise I'd made to Lizzy just before she was arrested.

2

I look into the eyes of my daughter. While Ev was pregnant, I imagined the moment I would first look into them. I wondered if it would be like when I looked into Matthew's eyes. They looked nothing like my son's eyes, though. Nothing about Madison reminds me of Matthew. They look, sound, and even smell different. Sometimes, I think it's a good thing she doesn't remind me of him. If she did, I would only be sad when I'm with her.

I place Madison on the blanket spread out on the nursery floor before lying next to her. I love Madison, but despite how much it pains me to admit, I've found it hard to bond with her. I feel guilty for that. We lost Matthew after only having him for a matter of hours, but the connection was instant. When I saw him in Lizzy's arms, it was like they were the only two people in the world, and suddenly, my life was complete. Then, as quick as I had it all, I lost it.

What kind of father doesn't bond with his child? I

warned Ev that I was damaged and the last person in the world she should try to make a happily ever after with. Sometimes, I wonder if it's the way Evelyn was while pregnant that led me to feel a lack of connection with Madison now. She was so different than anything I'd experienced with Lizzy. Lizzy was a goddess when it came to being pregnant. She adored every moment. She embraced her baby bump, and if she was home, she tended only to wear her sports bra and underwear. I loved it. I loved seeing how being a mother made her glow.

Evelyn had a rough pregnancy. By the second trimester, we'd stopped having sex because it made her sick. She refused to let me see her naked and never wanted me to touch her stomach. I was at every one of Lizzy's doctor appointments, but in contrast, Evelyn wouldn't tell me about them until after the fact. I was determined not to repeat my past mistakes, so I tried to give Evelyn space. I never imagined it would lead to me missing Madison's birth.

When my old college roommate, Vance, asked me to go to his bachelor party in Vegas, it was an easy no for me. We were only a month away from the baby's due date, and no way would I choose drinking with my buddies over being the husband Ev needed during that time. She insisted I go. She said I was being silly and we still had four weeks until the baby was due. She told me it would be my last chance for a guys' trip since being a father would take up my spare time soon enough.

I insisted that I stay home, but she revealed she wanted some alone time. Reluctantly, I agreed to go. I checked in frequently with her while I was away. She would let my calls go to voicemail and then text that she was working and would call me later. Eventually, it felt like a nuisance, so I stopped calling. I never imagined I'd find what I did when I got home. Evelyn wasn't waiting for me when I walked in. I'd called out her name, but there was no response, so I went to look for her.

When I walked into the nursery to find Evelyn rocking a baby in her arms, it didn't register at first what I was seeing. I even asked her whose baby it was.

"Yours, silly," she said after she laughed.

She told me how she'd gone into labor the morning before and that Madison was born within thirty minutes by the time she got to the hospital. She said she didn't want to ruin my trip. I was dumbfounded; then I was furious. Rather than ruin a trip I could have gone on at any time in my life, she chose to take away the birth of my child from me.

I never told her how much that hurt me, but even now, as I look into Madison's eyes, I can't help but wonder if all these things led up to why I struggle to feel the same bond with her that I felt with Matthew.

"I'm going to be better for you," I whisper to Madison as my fingers trail up and down her tummy. She wiggles under my touch and grunts in response.

3

The following day, the sound of the television wakes me up. I walk into the living room and stop when I hear the familiar intro song to the show Friends. It was Lizzy's favorite show to binge-watch. She watched the entire series from beginning to end twice while pregnant. She once told me that it was always what she imagined her life would be like after college. She would move to New York, find some roommates, have experiences, and date her way through the city searching for Mr. Right. She used to tell me I came along and ruined everything in the best way possible. She'd found Mr. Right before she graduated from college, and I'd stolen her big adventure. I promised her our lives would be an even grander adventure. I had been so wrong.

My eyes drift to Evelyn. She's staring at me as she holds Madison, who has a bottle to her lips. "Everything okay?" she asks me.

I nod. "Yeah, I didn't know you like this show."

"I don't," she grunts. "But Madison seems to."

I try not to reveal the memory it has stirred in me. "I'm heading to meet the real estate agent at the house." The house. It sounds wrong when I say it. It's home. Well, it was home. It was the home Lizzy and I had planned to raise our family in. For the past couple of years, it's been an empty tomb, though.

She sighs. "I'll be so glad when we are finally rid of that nightmare."

I can see how it's a nightmare for her. A past that will never go away as long as it exists. I suppose for me, it only holds ghosts these days. That is why when she suggested we get a place close to the hospital, I didn't resist. It made sense with the baby coming that we should live closer to Evelyn's work.

"Do you need anything while I'm out?" I ask, ignoring her comment.

"We could use more formula," she replies. I was surprised when Evelyn said she wasn't going to breast-feed, though her explanation made perfect sense. She planned to return to work right away and needed to focus on her patients and not worry about pumping constantly. Lizzy couldn't wait to breastfeed. It broke my heart that Matthew was too weak to even latch on. She never got to have that experience with our son. I told myself it was a personal decision that I had no business having an opinion about and Evelyn owed me no explanation. Trying not to compare the two of them has been more challenging than I ever thought it would be.

I turn toward the door and scoop up the keys into my hand, pausing when I hear Evelyn call after me.

"Nathan."

I step back into the room and look at my wife as she places our daughter over her shoulder and pats her back. "Yes, dear?" I smile as I say the words.

"Promise you'll be careful," she adds, looking at me with wide eyes.

"I always am," I reply as I turn to leave, but I know there is more to her statement. She's talking about Lizzy. She's warning me to watch out for my ex-wife. This is the life we live now. The life I have brought my wife and child into, worrying that my unstable ex-wife could harm them. Especially with the new evidence, I have doubts that Lizzy murdered Alison, but I do know she stalked her. She stalked us. She watched us having sex on cameras she placed in Alison's home. No matter what feelings may linger for Lizzy, she needs help, and I won't be so naïve as to think she doesn't pose a threat to my new family.

When I pull the door closed behind me, I check the handle to ensure it's locked.

4

The memory of the day I surprised Lizzy with this house pushes at the edges of my thoughts as I sit in front of it. I remind myself that just as many nightmarish memories exist in that home. The ones of all the nights we wept together after each lost pregnancy. We told each other lies as we pretended everything would be okay between us. Then there was the night my wife was placed in the back of a police car.

This perfect Tudor in the pristine affluent neighborhood wasn't my home for a long time. It became an image in the news. The house where the wife who murdered her husband's mistress plotted the evil deed. The internet was a wasteland of ignorant people spewing things they knew nothing about.

In the end, though, the police had evidence of what Lizzy had done. She didn't deny it in the trial. She admitted she stalked us and planned the murder, but not once did she waver in denying she committed the crime. I found it easier to believe the media and the version of the facts they put out than to believe the words out of my wife's mouth. Now, after the retrial and the missed DNA evidence that came to light, Lizzy is free. The new jury was convinced there was reasonable doubt regarding the case.

I wonder as I exit the car and make my way up the walkway to the entrance and slide the key into the front door. Am I convinced? Does it matter anymore if I'm convinced? I made my choice when I married Evelyn.

I never told Evelyn that I don't remember sleeping with her. I decided it would serve no purpose other than to serve no purpose other than to hurt her. Sometimes, I feel like I don't remember when we began dating. She subtly moved from friend to a more constant companion, then I found out she was pregnant.

I push the thoughts out of my head because I know dwelling on the fact that I don't love Evelyn in the same way I did Lizzy will only cause me to pull away from her more. My mother was the other woman, and I was the secret the two of them had. He was wealthy and married, so I was my father's dirty little secret. I never want my daughter to feel unwanted the way I had as a child. I can't deny that Evelyn is good for me. She's grounded and logical; she tempers my impulsiveness. Since I destroyed my life with Lizzy, Evelyn and Madison are my last shot at happiness.

I stand at the grand entrance of the home I purchased as a gift to Lizzy. The memory of the way her eyes lit up when she first saw the large chandelier and how she ran her hand along the wood paneling as she traveled down the hall toward the kitchen hangs in my thoughts. I follow the path as if I'm chasing the memory.

Evelyn hasn't stayed a single night in this house. She hates coming here. She feels that when I'm here, it makes me sad, and she hates seeing me like that. Perhaps, she's right. I don't think we always know what we feel when we are in the middle of it. Sometimes, it's like a haze surrounding us, and we are in it for so long that we forget what normal is. I'm not even sure I remember what normal looked like for Lizzy and me. We tortured each other for so long that it had, in a way, become our new normal.

I've had a lot of time to think about what went wrong in my first marriage. I went numb. It wasn't just the pain of losing pregnancy after pregnancy or Matthew's death. It was constantly seeing the pain my wife was going through and not being able to soothe her. It wasn't because I didn't want to or hadn't tried. It was as if she wanted to be in that pain. When I would attempt to comfort her, it only made her angry, like I was trying to rob her of something she felt was hers and hers alone.

Tossing the house keys on the kitchen counter, I make my way up the stairs to the master suite. I sit on the end of the bed I'd shared with Lizzy. Evelyn suggested I sell the home in turnkey condition. She thought even an item of furniture would be a reminder of my life before her, and if our new family was ever going to have a chance of flourishing, I needed to let go of it all.

She isn't wrong. As I sit on the bed, a memory of Lizzy in a sexy red dress pops into my mind. The way the fabric slid to the side and revealed her thigh. I feel myself grow hard with the memory. I stand, fleeing the past. I make my way to the window overlooking the backyard. The pool is covered now, and I notice how lonely it looks with the fallen leaves blown across it. Lizzy loved the pool. I did too, mostly because she liked being naked in the pool. I remember the way her pregnant stomach glistened as the water beaded on it.

"Dammit," I mutter to myself, frustrated by the memories that plague me. I glance at my phone, checking the time. The real estate agent should be here soon. A movement in the courtyard catches my attention. My gaze focuses on the bench near the hydrangea bushes. My breath catches in my throat as my eyes fixate on the back of the blond head. It's like I can fucking see her, I think as I stare at the ghostly image.

I begin to shake when she stands and turns toward the house, staring up at me. Our eyes meet, and I realize it's not a memory. Lizzy is standing in our courtyard. She's here, at our home, and I'm looking right at her. My heart starts pounding in my chest as we continue staring at each other. She doesn't move, and I wonder if she can see me through the window. Does she know I'm looking back at her? Her lips turn up into the slightest of smiles. She sees me. She must.

What's she doing here? Panic floods my thoughts, and I remember the recent revelation from Evelyn. Lizzy threatened my wife. I can't imagine her threatening Evelyn, but I also could never have envisioned her stalking Alison. I need to talk to her.

Turning, I race out the double doors of our master suite and down the stairs. I'm out of breath as I approach the back doors and throw them open. I dart around the pool to where I had seen Lizzy standing just moments ago, but she's gone. My head jerks around as I search for her, frantic now.

"Liz?" I call out, but there is no answer. "I know you're here."

She's not, though. There is no trace of her. Did I imagine it all? I walk to the bench, and my blood runs cold when I spot a small blue box sitting on it. My feet are heavy as I walk to it. Staring, I will myself forward, terrified of what I will find inside. With an exhale, I flip the lid to the box off with a single finger.

Reaching inside, I pull out a silver baby rattle engraved with the name Foster. I recognize it instantly as the gift I purchased for our child. Lizzy and I wanted a house full of kids, so I wanted our last name on the rattle to pass it on from one sibling to the next. An heirloom our children would pass on to our grandchildren one day. But we only had one child, and he was gone the day we met him. My eyes grow wet as I clutch the rattle to my chest. I'm drowning in the pain of the memory, each breath harder than the last to draw in and out.

I look around again, half expecting to see Lizzy standing behind me, but I'm alone. She was here, though. The rattle proves I didn't imagine it. Why would she have left this here for me? I wonder.

My thoughts shift to Evelyn and Madison, alone in the condo together, and panic fills me. I shove the rattle in my pocket and take off in a sprint, back through the house to my car. The real estate agent drives up next to me as I pull open my door.

"Mr. Foster?" she questions through her rolled-down window. "I'm not late, am I?"

I shake my head, not slowing down. "I'm sorry, my wife needs me home right away," I reply. "The front door is unlocked, and the keys are on the kitchen counter. Email me anything else you need."

"Oh . . ." She gasps and seems confused, but I don't have time to explain. I need to get home and make sure my family is safe.

5

I try calling Evelyn repeatedly on the way home. No answer. I consider calling a neighbor to check on her and Madison but then realize I don't know any of our neighbors' numbers. Once I pull into the reserved parking spot of our building, I waste no time exiting my car and racing up to the condo building's security door to press in my passcode.

After I enter, I repeatedly push the elevator button, impatiently waiting for the doors to open. We live here because it's a safe building with security cameras everywhere. It's a secure entrance, and a key card is required to activate the elevator. There's no way Lizzy could get to Ev and the baby, but I can't seem to calm my racing heart. I redial Ev, and it goes straight to voicemail.

When I reach our floor, I waste no time rushing to our door and shoving the key into the lock. Within seconds, I'm inside and searching for my family. "Ev?" I call out. I call out again, more frantic, now louder, "Evelyn?" I'm in the kitchen, looking into the living room, where I had left Ev watching Friends, but she's no longer there.

I turn around to check our bedroom when she emerges from the hallway. "What is wrong with you?" she hisses. "I just got Madison to sleep," she warns in a strained whisper.

I stop and rest against the edge of the island. I notice how quiet the condo is, and I attempt to slow my breathing.

"I tried to call you," I answer in a low voice.

"My phone is on the couch. I have it silenced because I was putting Madison down," she explains, obviously irritated. "What is wrong with you?"

I shake my head, not wanting to alarm her. "Nothing. Just when you didn't answer, I got worried."

She studies my face for a moment, and I can see that she recognizes the concern in my eyes. She closes the space between us and reaches out to place a hand on my arm. "What aren't you telling me?"

"Nothing. Everything's fine." I feel silly for overreacting. Forcing a smile, I slide off my coat. When I move past her to hang the coat in the entry closet, it knocks against the wall, making a noise.

Her brows stitch together in confusion. "What was that noise?"

I consider pretending it's nothing for a moment but then remind myself that honesty is part of being a better man. Secrets were what destroyed Lizzy's and my marriage. I reach into the pocket of my jacket, and without a word, I pull out the silver baby rattle I had hidden in there. I watch Evelyn's face. Her eyes widen.

"Is that for me?" she asks, a smile pulling at the corners of her mouth. It disappears when I shake my head.

"What is it?" she inquires.

"I found it at the house."

"What house?" she asks, realizing the answer before I have time to offer it. "I don't understand. What do you mean you found it at the house?" She follows up with another question.

"I think Lizzy was there."

"What?" She gasps before stumbling back a couple of steps. "Did you speak to her?"

I shake my head again. "I think I saw her out the window in the courtyard. By the time I got out there, though, she was gone. I found this rattle sitting on a bench where she had been."

Her head bobs, and I can tell she is both concerned and confused. "Why would she leave a baby rattle?"

"I had gotten it for our son," I explain. "I don't know. Maybe it was her way of saying goodbye."

"Her way of saying goodbye? I know you're not that stupid." Panic is evident in Evelyn's voice.

"Excuse me?" I snap, anger swelling in my gut.

"I knew she wouldn't just move on. I told you she wouldn't be happy until she has you back," Evelyn hisses, and I feel like there is an accusation behind her words.

"You're jumping to conclusions," I huff as I push past Evelyn and make my way down the hall to the living room.

"We are not done with this conversation, Nathan," she says, chasing after me.

Turning on my heel, I glare at her, then remind myself of the promise I made to my daughter before she was even born. I promised to try to be a better man for her. Sucking in a deep breath, I release it slowly in an effort to calm myself before I reply. At last, I say, "I don't think that's why she was there."

"She was at your house!" Evelyn no longer seems concerned about being quiet for the baby.

"Think about this logically," I start. "If Liz wanted me back, wouldn't she have tried to talk to me? It doesn't make sense that she would have left the rattle for me to find and then run away before I got down there, if that was her intention."

Evelyn tosses her hands up in the air. "You're trying to apply logic to a person we know is irrational. Why was she there in the first place? That's not her home anymore."

"That's not fair," I insist. "It was her home before everything happened."

"Everything as in her going to prison for trying to kill your girlfriend?"

"You have to stop this," I demand. "Liz is out, and there's nothing we can do about it. Either you trust me or you don't."

"This has nothing to do with trust! This is about keeping our child safe."

"Exactly! You have to trust that I'll keep Madison safe."

"I can't do this," Ev mutters before moving into the living room and starting to pace.

"What's that supposed to mean?"

She stops, then closes her eyes for a few seconds

before opening them and looking up at me. "I have to protect Madison."

"And you don't think I want to do the same thing?" Her words hurt me.

"Honestly, I don't know what you want," she states firmly. "I told you she threatened me, and here you are, defending her."

"I'm not defending her," I insist.

"What would you call it?" She's angry, and part of me thinks she's justified, while the other part of me is just pissed off at the world. I don't want to feel torn between my wife and ex-wife, but this is where I am now.

"What do you want me to do?" I ask, hoping she doesn't say she wants to involve the police. While I want to protect Ev and Madison, I don't want to land Liz back in prison. We filed a restraining order against her, and that's precisely what will happen if I involve the police. After everything she's been through, it doesn't seem right.

Evelyn looks out the window at the other high-rise across the street. I approach her slowly and place a hand on her back. When she doesn't pull away, I take that as a good sign.

"Just tell me. I'll do whatever you want me to," I offer, just wanting the argument to end.

Ev turns her head, and our eyes connect. "I want to move."

I shake my head in confusion. "I don't understand. We just moved to this building. Do you not like it here?" I ask. I wasn't fond of the idea of living in a condo and having neighbors on the other side of a wall, but I did it because that's what Evelyn wanted. The security in the building made her feel safe.

"No, I want to leave Boston," she reveals.

"What?" The word falls out of my mouth. I didn't see this coming. Evelyn has never mentioned wanting to move away from the city. Both our careers are here.

She pulls away from me and plops down onto the sofa. I take a seat next to her, confusion etched on my face. "It's not just that I don't feel safe from your ex. It's everything here."

"What do you mean?"

"When I was interviewing possible nannies, they all recognized our last name from the news."

"I know, but you found a solution to that," I argue. And she had.

"A solution?" Evelyn huffs. "Bridget doesn't want to be a nanny. She's only doing it until we can find someone else." Bridget is a nurse Ev knows from the hospital. She retired several months ago, and when Ev could not find a nanny she felt comfortable with, she reached out to Bridget.

"She seems to be happy enough with the job," I reply. "Have you talked to her about it again? Maybe things have changed, and she's willing to stay longer."

Evelyn groans in frustration. "Nathan, it's not only about the nanny. Everything in this city is a reminder of Liz and Alison." When she says Alison's name, I wince as the image of my murdered mistress flashes across my mind. "I want to be your wife. I want us to be a family. Madison, you, me."

"That's what I want too," I say, and I'm not lying. I

want us to be a family too. I just didn't realize it would be so hard for me to let go of Liz. It felt easier when she was in prison because she was the bad guy. I was allowed to hate her, to blame her for what happened to our lives. But now that she's been released and her guilt is not so clear, I find my feelings more muddled when it comes to Liz.

"Is it?" When she asks the question, I feel an ache in my chest. Am I this bad at relationships?

On paper, Evelyn should be everything I ever wanted. She's intelligent and beautiful. I mean, hell, she dedicates her life to helping people. I care about her. Maybe I even love her in some form, but she obviously can tell I am not all in. Liz has a part of me that I don't know if I will ever get back.

"You don't think I want to be with you and Madison?" I ask her pointedly.

She swallows, and I can tell she's measuring her words carefully. "If you want to be a family, this is your chance."

"So what are you saying? I agree to move, or it means I don't love you? That's insane."

"No, you move because if you love us like you say you do, you want to give us a chance. Let's start over, somewhere that nobody knows who we are." The anger in Evelyn's voice is gone, and all I hear now is desperation.

"What about my job?" Her suggestion is tempting. I've grown tired of being recognized in the line at the grocery store or finding news trucks parked at my work anytime something reignites the media's interest in Alison's murder.

"What about it? They took your major accounts away."

It stings when she points out the recent development at my office. It is true. The partners felt I was distracted with everything going on, and as a result, my work started to slip. My numbers were not what they should have been, and since I didn't bring in any new clients to the firm in over a year, they felt perhaps that was where my focus should be. The truth is I hate my job. I never feel fulfilled with it, but what the hell else can I do if I'm not a financial advisor? How can I support a family? What will my father say if I leave the firm?

I sigh. "I could ask to be transferred to the New York office."

"New York?" She shakes her head. "No, it'll just be more of the same."

"What does that mean?"

"It means they all know you. We'll still be in the same social circles we are now, and it will still be more of the same whispering behind our backs. Is that what you want for Madison? Do you want her to grow up with kids always talking about what happened with her dad's first wife?"

I shrug. "If not New York, then where?"

"Let's go somewhere that nobody knows who we are."

I laugh. "I'm not sure that place exists."

"We should try Michigan," she says, and I can tell this isn't some random suggestion. Evelyn already knows exactly where she wants us to go.

"What the hell is in Michigan?" I'm not sure I've ever even been to the state.

"Exactly!" she exclaims. "I've always wanted to live on a lake. Can't you just picture us in some small town where Madison can walk to school, and we attend community picnics and sit on our porch swing while she plays in the front yard?"

I never imagined such a life because the idea felt like a fantasy. I grew up in Boston as the son of a wealthy and influential man and his mistress. My example of family was nothing like the picture Evelyn described. That doesn't mean the thought isn't exciting. "I don't know what to say."

"Say you choose us," she pleads, staring at me, her eyes wet at the edges.

I reach out and place a hand on her leg, sad when I feel her stiffen under my touch.

"Of course, I choose you," I assure her. "But we have to be realistic. There is no way my firm would let me work remotely."

She shakes her head wildly. "So quit."

Her words surprise me, and I laugh softly. "And how exactly do you propose we live?"

"We have enough money. You don't need to work at that place. Take what we have saved and go start your own firm in Michigan," she suggests. "I can start a small practice out of the house, or maybe do something else."

"Ev, the money would be nothing like what we're used to," I say, actually somewhat excited about the idea of breaking away from it all—breaking away from my father. If we left Boston, no reminders of what happened to Alison would be staring me in the face. Lizzy would be forever part of my past. My stomach twists into knots as I think more about the reality of what she suggests. The part that excites me about leaving it all behind is the same thing that terrifies me. I care about Evelyn, but can I handle her being the only person in my life besides Madison? Will it help me grow fonder of her, or will it shine a spotlight on how incapable I am of being a loving husband to her?

"Can I think about it?" I ask.

Evelyn throws her arms around my neck and pulls me in closer, squealing in excitement. I don't get to see this side of her very often, and I like it. A smile stretches its way across her face. "Oh, Nathan. That's all I'm asking, my love. Think about it."

That isn't all she's asking, though. I can tell Evelyn is at the end of her rope. If I don't agree to the move, there's a serious chance I'll lose this new family. It won't be at the hands of Lizzy, but Evelyn when she takes our daughter and leaves me.

6

It's almost eleven when I finally get to work. Bridget had an emergency this morning. Her cocker spaniel ate an entire Hershey chocolate bar that her grandson left out when visiting. Since Evelyn had an early morning patient appointment, I hung out with Madison until Bridget finished her vet visit. I like when it's just Madison and me.

When I walk into the office, I head straight to the coffee pot since we ran out of grounds at our condo yesterday. Lizzy always took care of things like that in our marriage. I don't expect Ev to take care of the same things, but it is something we haven't worked out in our routine together. While thinking of it, I set a reminder on my calendar to pick up coffee grounds on the way home. Before I close the reminder, I add formula, remembering in my rush to get home after seeing Lizzy yesterday, how I forgot to stop and pick some up.

Lizzy's face fills my thoughts as I stand with the coffee pot in my hand. Why was she there? Why was she at the house? Why did she leave the rattle? Was she trying to say something to me? Send me a message? Or was it as simple as I suggested to Ev? She was there seeking closure. I wonder if she has as much trouble as I have letting go of us.

"You gonna pour the coffee or dance with it?" Brad, one of the partners at the firm, asks as he approaches from behind.

"I guess the baby is keeping me up at night more than I realize." I force a laugh. "Sorry about that." I grip a mug in my other hand and start to pour the coffee.

"The baby or the wife?" Brad teases as he jabs me in the ribs. I hate Brad. He is a complete asshole. Sometimes, I wonder if I started to turn into Brad when I cheated with Alison. I push the thought out of my head. I hate to think I could be anything like that prick.

"You got me there." My response is fake, but he doesn't notice. He's wrong, though. Evelyn and I do not have a relationship like that. There isn't passion. Honestly, if it wasn't for the drunken night that resulted in Madison, I'm not sure we would have ever moved into a physical relationship. Don't get me wrong, Evelyn isn't necessarily a lousy fuck. We just lack the passion I had with Lizzy. I thrive on that kind of primal connection. That's part of how I ended up sleeping with Alison in the first place. Lizzy was depressed—shit, we both were because we just buried our kid. The last thing she wanted was her husband pawing at her. If I had been the husband she needed me to be instead of the selfish asshole I was, maybe we would still be together, and maybe Alison would still be alive. So many what-ifs plague my thoughts these days.

"Just don't let the wife find out about that one." Brad chuckles as he nods his head in the direction of my office. A girl with long sandy-blond hair sits on my couch, but I don't recognize her. "Damn, Foster, you sure do like 'em young, you dog."

I force another grin, deciding it best not to explain to the Neanderthal who's my boss that I have no idea who the woman in my office is, and I certainly have no intention of repeating past mistakes by cheating on my new wife.

The girl taps her foot nervously as I head toward my door. She has a folder on her lap, so she must be here to apply for my assistant position. I've gone through at least half a dozen since Lizzy's trial started. Some left because they couldn't handle the constant harassment from the press. I had to dismiss others since they had only sought out the job because they were crime addicts, something I didn't know existed until I found myself in the middle of a case with national coverage.

I enter my office and close the door behind me. As I sit behind my desk, the girl looks uncomfortable. I immediately apologize and explain I had babysitter issues and was running behind.

"I promise, I don't bite," I tease, surprised the agency sent me someone so young, though it's likely they are running out of candidates. "Is that your résumé?" I ask, reaching out a hand across my desk.

She tightens her grip on the folder, and I notice she's trembling. Her voice cracks when she tries to speak, and she clears her throat. "I think there's been some sort of confusion. I'm not here to apply for a job."

"Who are you?" I ask, stiffening in my chair. Instantly, I think she's a reporter who got past security with a sweet face and a lie, but she seems too young for that.

"My name is Savannah," she replies, looking down at her lap. "Your wife helped me."

"Evelyn?" I ask, wondering how the girl found me.

She shakes her head. "I'm sorry, your ex-wife. Liz changed my life. She helped me find a new lawyer who was able to get me out of prison, and she connected me with people who could help me after I was out."

I study her for a moment. It feels odd that Lizzy has a life now that I'm not part of. I used to know everyone she knew. Now she's a stranger to me, just as this girl sitting in front of me is. "Apparently, figuring a way out of prison is something my ex is very good at," I reply coldly. "Now, can you please tell me what you're doing here, or should I go ahead and call security?"

"Liz asked me to come talk to you," she starts, but I cut her off.

"There is nothing my ex-wife has to say that I have any interest in hearing," I state firmly, making sure my voice is quiet enough that I don't draw the attention of my co-workers.

"I know you don't believe me, but Liz is trying to help you," Savannah replies. She takes a deep breath, and I see her grasp tighten even more on the folder in her hands. Her eyes are fixed on mine, and I see her jaw stiffen. The trembling and nervousness have disappeared, left with what I can only describe as a look of disgust.

"I doubt that," I snap.

She rolls her eyes. "I don't know why she even bothers with you. You don't deserve it."

This girl has no idea how right she is. I never deserved a wife like Liz. Maybe that's why I lost her.

"Yeah, well, you tell Liz to stay away from my family, do you hear me?"

She bites her lip, and I can tell she's trying to stop herself from unleashing fury on me. She swallows hard before she continues. "You're not safe."

I lean forward, hoping my body language comes across as menacing to the young girl. "Are you threatening me?"

"No, of course not." She scoffs.

"You need to leave," I demand, standing and pointing at the door.

She stands as well. "You are such an idiot."

"I can tell you've been talking to my ex-wife." I chuckle after I make the statement.

"You think this is funny?" She hurls the question at me.

I'm suddenly deadly serious in my tone. "I have a terrified wife and new baby at home, so no, I don't think any part of this is funny."

Savannah rubs her face in exhaustion. "I don't know how to tell you this, but your supposedly terrified wife at home is not who you think she is."

"Excuse me?" I gasp, not hiding my anger. "Don't you dare say a word about Evelyn."

"Whatever, I'm only here as a favor to Liz," the girl continues as she inches closer to the door. She's scared even though she's trying to act like she's not. I doubt she can be much older than twenty.

"You need to get out of here, or I will call the police," I threaten, though I have no intention of following through. "And you should be more careful about the people you're choosing to hang out with."

She's shaking her head, her face has turned a bright shade of red, and she's vibrating with anger. She growls in frustration. "I told her there was no way you'd listen to me. She said if you knew she sent me, you would hear me out, but it's so obvious, you never loved her."

I have to fight the urge to defend my feelings for Liz. Not only did I love Liz more than any woman I ever have, I still do. I hate myself for it. I have a new family now. "Fine," I snap. "Say what you came here to say."

She looks at me as if she's afraid I may strike her if she approaches me. I soften my posture, and she inches toward me, handing me the envelope she had been gripping in her hand, before backing up to the door again.

"What's this?" I ask, glancing down at it.

"Inside that envelope are copies of all the letters Evelyn sent to Liz while she was in prison," she explains.

I shake my head. "I don't understand. Why are you giving me these?"

"Liz thought if you read through them, you could help spot inconsistencies in Evelyn's story. If we can find a starting point, that can help us so much."

"Inconsistencies? What in the hell are you talking about?" My patience is thin again.

"Evelyn killed Alison," she blurts out, then stands there, frozen, looking at me expectantly. "You can help us prove that Liz is innocent." I look back at her, processing her statement with a confused look.

"You want me to help prove my ex-wife is innocent by helping you prove my wife is a killer?" I repeat the scenario, assuming I must be misunderstanding what she's saying.

"I know she's the mother of your child but doesn't it bother you knowing that she's the one who killed Alison?"

"You're crazy. Liz is crazy." I am shouting without warning.

"You have to listen to me. Evelyn's not who you think she is," Savannah continues. I stride across the room, but she doesn't budge. Gripping her arm, I throw open the door and drag her past all the cubicles with everyone's eyes plastered on us. I don't care who sees this anymore. She needs to leave. She continues with her insane accusations, but I don't reply. Finally, I reach the security guard and promptly hand her off.

"This girl is trespassing, and if you see her here again, I want you to call the police," I instruct the guard, who immediately apologizes and assures me he will take care of the matter.

I turn to walk away, and the girl shouts after me, "If you don't listen to Liz, you will end up regretting it."

I stop dead in my tracks, which causes the guard to hesitate. I turn and approach her, now only inches from her face. "You tell Liz if she or anyone else comes near my family or me again, I won't hesitate to put them in the ground."

I see the guard shift uncomfortably from the corner

of my eye before he pulls Savannah behind him and out the doors. I watch through the glass until I can't see them anymore and then turn and head back, trying my best to ignore all the people who are staring.

I enter my office and close my door. Maybe Evelyn is right, and moving is the only way Madison will ever have a shot at everyday life. I take the envelope containing the letters Evelyn wrote to Liz and place it into my shredder without hesitation. It's time I leave the past exactly where it belongs.

7

I 've never told Evelyn, but I don't like to see her at her work. For me, the color of the walls, the smell, and the beeping of the monitors all bring me back to the day I lost my son. Losing the other pregnancies was hard, but losing Matthew after watching him being born, getting to spend hours with him, watching him move, his eyelids flutter, and his little hand grip Lizzy's finger . . . The hospital where we were forced to say goodbye to him holds nothing but pain for me.

After the things I did to the people in my life, I don't deserve happiness, but somehow, I have Madison. I have another chance at being a dad, but it doesn't make what I lost any easier to cope with.

The doors close behind me, and I'm immediately hit with hospital smells. Matthew and Lizzy invade my thoughts, and I remind myself why I'm here. I think of the visit I received from Lizzy's prison mate at work. I'm here to surprise my wife with the news I'm on board with moving away from Boston. Boston is all I have known, but familiarity can't be a reason to stay. When I stop and break down my memories of this city, the ones that make me smile are of my mother, who is no longer alive, and Lizzy before everything went so wrong. Why would I cling to this place that holds so much pain for the people around me and myself? My father is here, but that would be more of an argument to flee if anything. He never openly claimed me as his, yet his ever-watchful eyes are always on me. Lizzy hated his control over our lives when he wasn't an active participant. If I stay in Boston, will Evelyn eventually feel the same way? My father hasn't asked to meet Madison, though I can't say I'm surprised, considering he didn't attend his grandson's funeral.

My face is hot, thinking of my father, as I enter the elevator and press the button that leads to Evelyn's floor. There was a time I wasn't that different from him. I swore I would never cheat on my wife, but I did. And when Alison told me she was pregnant, I felt like my entire world was crumbling. I was just like the old man. I loved Lizzy. I regretted straying, but I couldn't change what I had done. Alison was going to have my child, and I would have to face the consequences. I tried to figure out a way to tell Lizzy about the affair and the baby when they discovered Alison's body. I was going to beg for Lizzy's forgiveness. Offer to go to counseling, whatever she wanted, if only she would take me back. I would be in the life of Alison and my child, but I wanted Lizzy to be part of it too. I didn't know what her response would be. I was almost sure she would hate me and immediately file for divorce, but all I knew was I didn't want to be another version of my father.

It doesn't matter now, I think as the elevator doors open. Evelyn is right. I need to put my family first and get us out of Boston. I walk down the long hall, suddenly wishing I bought flowers before I came. Romantic gestures came so easy to me with Lizzy. We were madly in love with each other, at least for most of our marriage. It doesn't come naturally with Evelyn. I was honest with her after that drunken night of sex. I told her it was a mistake and I was sorry I allowed things to get out of control. When she told me she was pregnant, I told her she didn't need to worry because I would be there for the baby. That's when Evelyn suggested getting married.

I wasn't on board at first. I told her she deserved to have someone who loved her in a way I didn't. Evelyn is a very logical person and argued that statistically, Madison's best chance at a happy life was with a mom and dad in the same home. Somehow, she convinced me that love would grow between us over time.

I round the corner and find myself standing in front of Evelyn's door. I'm surprised when I see the nameplate next to the door. Dr. Evelyn Foster. I'm unsure if the updated nameplate is recent or if I simply hadn't noticed it on previous visits. It hadn't crossed my mind that she'd take my last name professionally. It feels foreign as I stare at the letters. Evelyn is my wife, but somehow, it feels like we're playing pretend.

"Are you here to see Dr. Foster?" a voice asks from behind me, and I stiffen when I hear the name.

I turn and smile at a young nurse approaching. "Yes, I'm—" I start before she interrupts.

"Mr. Foster!" she squeals, rushing up to me and grabbing my arm. "Oh my gosh, it's so nice to meet you. From the way Dr. Foster is always going on and on about you, I feel like I already know you." She giggles. I wonder how she knows what I look like. I also can't imagine Evelyn talking about me or our marriage.

"Oh . . ." I gasp, trying to hide any look of surprise. I feel a twinge of guilt, considering most people at my office don't know I remarried. "Nice to meet you."

"Sherri," she interjects.

"Sherri," I add with a nod. "Is my wife here?"

She exaggerates a frown before she replies, "Oh, you just missed her. She was called out on a patient evaluation."

Evelyn doesn't talk about her work when she's home. I don't press her much on the subject because I can only imagine how heavy a mental toll her job must take. If she wants to talk about it, I assume she'll bring it up.

I tilt my head and shove my hands into my pockets. "Well, that's what I get for trying to surprise her."

Sherri beams a smile at me. "Aw, you are just as romantic as she says." I'm starting to think Sherri might have me mixed up with someone else. "Do you want to wait for her in her office?"

I consider the offer. "Do you know how long she'll be?"

"Sorry, I don't." She frowns again, and I'm suddenly uncomfortable with how overly expressive Sherri's facial muscles are.

"Do you think I can leave her a note?" I ask.

"Of course, silly," Sherri chimes cheerfully as she

reaches past me and opens the door. "It would make her day, I'm sure."

I thank Sherri for the help and step inside Evelyn's office. I've met Evelyn at work before, but as I peer around the room, I realize this is the first time I've been beyond the hallway outside of her office.

My initial thought is how sad the space is. There is a wall of locked filing cabinets to my left. In front of me are two chairs and behind that is Evelyn's desk. The majority of light comes from the window on the far side of the room. I flip the light switch and hear the hum of a fluorescent as it warms up overhead. It's small. There are no plants and no art on the walls. Lizzy had decorated my office at work, and I was relieved to have a sanctuary to work from.

I make my way around the desk and am not surprised when I find it well organized. Evelyn likes everything to be in its place at the condo. Our kitchen cabinets are filled with clear containers that she sorts our groceries in. I don't know where she finds the time, but the woman has a label on almost everything in the house. I look around her desk and try to think of where she would logically keep pen and paper. I open the middle drawer, and sure enough, a clear tray sits inside with all of the desk items sorted neatly, including pens. I grab one and pull open the drawer to my left to search for paper.

I reach in and lift out a pile of mail, setting it on the desk before finding a pad of paper hidden underneath where the mail had been. I pull it out and remove the top sheet before replacing it. Knowing that Evelyn will be annoyed if I do not return everything exactly as I found it,

I scoop up the mail from the desk and return it to the drawer. An envelope falls to the floor. I reach down and grab it, and as I place it on top, the return address catches my attention. Georgia.

Evelyn is from Georgia, though I don't know much about her life there. She isn't big on talking about her past, but I can't blame her. My past isn't exactly my favorite subject either. I pick the letter up to inspect it more closely. My chest tightens when I notice the name on the top left corner of the envelope. A. Powell. It was Evelyn's father's name. I stare at it, trying to understand why Evelyn would have a letter from her father, who died when she was in high school. The date stamped on the envelope is from a month ago, so that doesn't make sense.

Taking a seat in Evelyn's chair, I pull the letter back out of the drawer and stare at it. There has to be some explanation. I study the envelope torn open along the top, debating if I should read the letter tucked inside. It isn't mine to read. I swore I'd be a better man, a better husband. It's not my right to snoop into Evelyn's things. But she lied. The realization hangs all around me. Would I be wrong to read the letter, knowing she's hiding things from me? This isn't something small. Telling me her father is dead when he clearly isn't is a considerable mistruth.

As I stare at the envelope, trying to decide if I should read the letter, I think of that morning and the warning from Savannah. Is Evelyn not who I think she is? I can't deny that she's hiding things from me now. What else is she hiding from me? I pound a fist on the desk in frustration before tossing the letter on top of the pile of mail, then slam the drawer closed. I replace the pen in the top drawer and crumple up the piece of paper I had retrieved to write a note, tossing it in the trash. Before I leave, I slide Evelyn's chair in, leaving everything precisely as I had found it.

I'm not going to let Lizzy get inside my head. I will not let her destroy my new chance at a family. I will leave, and it will be like I never saw the letter. If Evelyn lied about her father, there has to be a reason. I know more than anyone how much a terrible father can completely screw up your life. Everyone has secrets, and it's not fair to think Evelyn doesn't have some of her own. I flip the light off and close the door behind me. I won't speak of my visit to her office when I see Evelyn tonight. I also won't bring up the move. I have to understand why Evelyn is hiding things from me before I agreed to move our entire lives, even if I know leaving Boston is the right thing to do.

8

The following day, I'm late getting to the golf course. Traffic is a nightmare, but Travis assumes it's because of the baby when I arrive. He mentions that I look tired, but Madison isn't why I'm losing sleep. I can't sleep because I know about Evelyn's secret. She lied to me about her father being dead.

Since the trial, this golf game has become a ritual with Travis every Wednesday morning. He's married with two small children at home, and I like that he seems to enjoy being a family man. I also like that he never asks questions about Lizzy or what happened. I eventually shared everything with him, which surprised even me. I don't share things about myself and certainly not with co-workers. For some reason, though, I trust Travis. He doesn't come from money, like most of my co-workers. There's an approachability about him that I find refreshing.

"So, any word on the Bishop account?" Travis asks as he steps up to tee.

"Yeah, that's not going to happen," I scoff.

He swings the club, watches the ball, then turns to look at me. "Man, you were the golden boy before . . ." Travis stops his words, and an uncomfortable silence hangs between us.

"Well, I'm not anymore," I correct as we walk toward the golf cart. "They've taken most of my major accounts already, so I seriously doubt I'm even in the running for the Bishop account."

"That's such bullshit," Travis grunts.

"Maybe," I say, then debate if I should say more. "Or maybe it's for the best."

"What's that supposed to mean?" Travis asks as he turns the cart, searching for the exact location of his ball.

"I mean . . ." I stop myself, questioning if saying anything would be a huge mistake. "Never mind, it's nothing."

Travis stops the cart after sensing my hesitation and turns to look at me. "What's going on?"

"I shouldn't say anything," I reply, even though I hope he'll continue to push.

"You wouldn't have brought it up if you didn't want to talk about it," he states, and I am again reminded of why I like Travis.

"I'm thinking about leaving the firm," I admit. Saying it out loud for the first time feels like I am suddenly lighter. I thought I would be sad to end this chapter of my life, but I realize nothing could be further from the truth. Evelyn was right. I do hate my job.

He blinks at me repeatedly as he processes my revelation, and I can see I shocked him. "Like leave, as in not work there anymore?" he asks at last.

I snort. "Well, yeah, that's kinda what leaving means."

He shakes his head. "This cock-blocking shit is only temporary, man. You just have to be patient. They'll give you back the keys to the kingdom, eventually."

The tension in my chest starts to release. It feels good to unburden myself of this secret. "That's not why I'm thinking of leaving."

"So why?" he asks, stepping out of the cart and approaching his ball. My ball is already on the green, so I wait for him to take his swing and return to the cart before explaining.

"Have you heard that my ex was released from prison?" I ask as we head toward the green.

He keeps his eyes focused on the path when he replies, "It's hard not to hear about it since it's all over the news. But I'm sure it will blow over eventually."

"I suppose." I hesitate, wondering if the trust I have placed in Travis is a mistake. Deciding I have nothing to lose, I drop the bomb and wait for him to process it. "My ex sent someone to the office to see me."

He stops the cart to the left of the green, and we both step out and approach our balls before he continues. "What do you mean when you say she sent someone?"

I sigh. "I got to work, and this woman was waiting for me inside my office."

"Well, that sounds terrifying."

"I went in and spoke to her, and she explained she had known my ex-wife in prison and that Lizzy had helped her find a lawyer to get her out."

"Wait, so she was like a felon?"

I shrug. "I mean, I guess."

"What did she look like?"

"Huh?" I ask, confused.

"I mean, did she have tattoos and everything?"

I laugh. "Trav, man, you have to stop shaping your view of the world from what you see on television."

"Sorry, I don't exactly have a ton of experience with people in prison," he grumbles before making a perfect putt.

"And I do?" I have more than he has, though. Lizzy was just like anyone else, and after a few wrong turns, she found herself on the other side of those fences. Some of the people in prison are just people whose mistakes caught up with them. In a way, I always thought I had deserved to be in there more than Liz.

He shrugs but doesn't say anything.

"She was young and seemed sweet from the limited interaction I had with her," I say, recalling my conversation with Savannah.

"What did she say?"

"That she was there because my ex wanted to warn me about Evelyn."

"Evelyn," he repeats. "As in your wife?"

Travis doesn't know Evelyn except for what I share with him. We didn't have a large wedding. We went to the courthouse to get married. She doesn't like to come to the office because she feels like everyone will stare at her. I can't blame her. It must be hard to marry someone with a past like mine.

"Yeah, she claimed Lizzy sent her."

Travis shakes his head before watching as I putt my ball into the hole. "Wait, I'm so confused. Your ex-wife and your new wife know each other?" Travis attempts to clarify.

"Evelyn ran my grief group." I share a lot with Travis, but I have not shared everything. We retrieve our balls from the final cup and take a seat in the cart, heading in the direction of the clubhouse.

"Yeah, I remember you telling me that's where you met."

"After Lizzy was found guilty, I was in a terrible place. That's about the time I started to let my work fall off."

"I mean, nobody can blame you, man," Travis offers. "I can't even imagine what you were going through."

I force a thankful smile before I continue, "At some point, Evelyn became more than a counselor to me. She could see I was hurting, and she just wanted to be there for me. She tried to help me move on from Lizzy, but I couldn't face it. She encouraged me to get a divorce as a step toward putting my past behind me."

Travis narrows his gaze. "I still don't understand how they know each other."

"Well, I told Evelyn I agreed with her and probably did need to file for a divorce. But I wanted to ask for it face-to-face, and I wasn't ready to see Lizzy yet." I pause as we pull into a spot in front of the clubhouse. "So Evelyn went to see Lizzy."

"Wait, you asked your girlfriend to see if she could get your wife to grant you a divorce?" Travis interrupts.

"God no," I answer. "I had no idea Evelyn and Lizzy

were talking until several weeks after they started meeting."

"What do you mean meeting?"

"Evelyn told me Liz had offered her a deal. She would give me an uncontested divorce if Evelyn would come to see her every week and let her tell her side of what happened."

"And you had no idea?"

I shake my head, and Travis huffs.

"What?"

"You must have been so pissed."

"Yeah, I can't believe after everything Lizzy did she would try to pull Evelyn into it."

"No," he interjects. "Pissed at Evelyn."

"Why would I be pissed at her? She was trying to help me."

"Look, man, I know she's your wife and all, but that is seriously fucked up that she would go talk to your ex like that without even asking you."

"I was pretty angry at first, but then when I confronted Evelyn about it, she broke down sobbing and told me how sorry she was and she was just trying to help," I tell him of the night Evelyn and I had our first fight. What I don't tell him is I thought things were over. I told Evelyn that night that I didn't want to see her again. The next time I saw her, she told me she was pregnant.

"You're a way more forgiving guy than I am," he huffs, lifting his brows in disbelief.

I shrug. "She told me before she realized what was happening, she was in over her head, and Lizzy was threatening she would tell me about the visits to break us up."

He shakes his head. "I mean, I guess it's good you guys figured it out. Now you have a baby and everything."

I smile but don't say anything in response.

"So this girl at your office," Travis continues, redirecting the conversation. "You said she came to you with a warning about Evelyn?"

"Yeah." I laugh awkwardly. "She had some crazy idea that I'm not safe and that Evelyn killed Alison."

"Okay." Travis lifted his hands into the air, signaling for me to stop. "Slow down. Now, I'm baffled. Evelyn also knew Alison?"

"No, that's just it. There's no way it could be true. I didn't meet Evelyn until after Lizzy's trial was over. The accusation is crazy. It's impossible."

"Then why would your ex send someone to tell you that?"

"I don't know. Because she's crazy?" I say.

"I thought they released her because of evidence that pointed to a new suspect," Travis attempts to clarify again.

"Yeah, well, I'm not so convinced she's innocent." When I say the words, I wonder if he can tell I'm lying. I was so convinced Lizzy did it, but now, I don't know what to think. She never changed her story. She admitted to all the terrible things she had done in stalking Alison, but she swore she did not kill her. After the new evidence came to light, I started to wonder if she was telling the truth, though I couldn't tell Evelyn or anyone else that. I'm with Evelyn now. People might think I still love Lizzy if I take her side.

"I don't understand why she would say that about Evelyn if there's no way she could have even known Alison," Travis says again.

"Hell, if I know. Evelyn has some crazy theory that Liz has some plan to try get me back."

"But you have a baby now," Travis states.

"And that's exactly why I'm thinking about leaving the firm. Evelyn is terrified of running into my ex one day. She also thinks that living in Boston could end up making Madison's life harder."

"I mean, she's not wrong," Travis agrees. "Sorry. I can't even imagine what that kid's going to hear growing up."

"Evelyn wants us to move away and cut all ties to this place."

"Is that what you want?"

"I want to be a good dad." When I say the words out loud, my chest tightens.

"I get that," Travis replies. Another reason I like him. "My kids are everything to me."

I look at him. "But I can't stop thinking about what that girl in my office said."

"What, that Evelyn is a killer? You said that's crazy. There's no way she even knew Alison."

"No, not that part," I say. "She said Evelyn isn't who I think she is."

"I mean, are any of us who we pretend to be?" Travis asks, trying to comfort me.

I shake my head and look around, ensuring no one is within earshot. "I'm going to sound crazy even saying this out loud."

"What is it?" he asks, his eyes alert as he waits for my response.

"I stopped by to see Evelyn at her work yesterday, and I found a letter in her desk from her father."

"Okay, did it say something disturbing?" Travis shook his head in confusion.

"I didn't read it," I admit.

"You lost me again."

"Evelyn told me her dad is dead," I reveal.

"What?"

"But the letter was recent. She lied to me."

Travis slumps back in his seat, mulling over what I just told him. "Why would she lie to you about her dad dying?"

"I have no idea."

"Did you ask her about it?"

"No," I exclaim, tossing my hands up into the air. "I don't want her to think I was snooping around in her desk."

"Were you?"

"No!" I defend myself. "I was going to write her a note that I stopped by to see her and I was thinking about what she had said about wanting to move, and I'm willing to consider it. It was just sitting there, on the top of a pile of mail in her drawer."

"What are you going to do?" Travis asks.

"I don't know." I shrug.

"Can I ask you a question, and it's okay if you punch me right in the face after I do?" he asks, leaning back a little after he says the words.

I laugh. "I don't know. With that kind of intro, I'm not

sure I'm up for it, but I guess so."

"Do you love Evelyn?"

My brows narrow at him. Travis has never asked me something as personal or as invasive as this question. I assumed if a man marries a woman, most people will obviously conclude he loves her. I, in fact, am not in love with Evelyn, though, so the assumption is incorrect if someone makes it. I care for her, which I don't think is precisely nothing.

"What kind of question is that?" I grunt. "I love my family."

He shakes his head. "No, of course, you love your daughter. I would never question that. What I asked is: do you love your wife?"

"I don't see what bearing that has on anything," I reply, not sure why I don't lie to him. Perhaps I view my conversations with him as sacred, a sort of confessional.

"Because if you love your wife, I doubt you would think about what your crazy ex suggests. You certainly wouldn't have a problem asking her about some stupid letter in her office that is probably just a misunderstanding," Travis explains. "But if there's a chance you don't love your wife, maybe what is bothering you is that you are worried there's a chance Liz is right about her."

"Are you crazy?" I snap. "Of course, I am not worried about that." Evelyn was no murderer.

Travis bursts out laughing and pushes me in the arm. "You should have seen your face. I really had you going." I laugh hesitantly as if I am not sure I understand the joke. "Dude, everyone knows you love your wife, and come on, you said it yourself. She never met Liz or Alison before you met her. Liz is messing with you."

"Do you think that's what this is?" I ask, actually hopeful at the idea.

"She goes to prison, and when she gets out, you have a new happy family, and you are selling the house the two of you had. I'm sure she's hella pissed and trying to get even," Travis adds. "So, what are you going to do about the move?"

My phone buzzes, and I look at the screen. It's a text from Evelyn asking if I have made it to the office yet. I slide the phone back into my pocket.

"I don't know. I'm thinking about doing it, though, for Madison's sake." I turn and look at him pointedly. "You can't tell anyone until after I make up my mind, though."

"I swear, your secret is safe with me," he says. I believe him. I hope that's not a mistake. I can tell he wants to say something else. As the silence grows between us, I look at him, and he finally speaks. "I'm no expert on marriage, but if you want it to work, my wife and I have no secrets from each other."

"Are you saying I should tell her Lizzy sent someone to see me?" I ask.

"Oh hell no, I didn't say do something crazy." He laughs. "All I'm saying is if my wife lied to me about her father being dead, I would want to know why."

9

I couldn't shake what Travis said at the end of our conversation. It stuck with me the entire day, and now, on the drive home, I decide to talk to Evelyn tonight. I can't let it fester. I need to understand why she would hide that her dad is still alive. If we are going to try to build a life together, I need to trust her.

After parking in my usual spot of our condo parking garage, I sit and run through different ways to bring up what I discovered in the desk drawer of Evelyn's office. I play out all the different ways she might respond in my imagination. I don't know how to predict Evelyn's reaction, though. I always knew the outcome of a conversation with Lizzy, even in the darkest depths of her depression, but Evelyn is much more calculating with her words. I often find I have trouble reading her emotions.

Slipping the key into the lock of our entry door, I open it and then close it behind me once I'm inside. Evelyn steps out of Madison's room before I set my bag down, bouncing our daughter up and down gently. She motions to me with a single finger to be quiet, and I obey, placing my items on the nearby hook and table with extreme delicacy. She turns back into the nursery, and I step into the doorway to watch her as she places our sleeping daughter into her crib.

Madison has been a sound sleeper since she came home from the hospital. I'm almost certain most babies are not the same, and I wonder what kind of baby Matthew would have been for a fleeting second. Evelyn tightens the blankets around Madison before tiptoeing from the room. She shoos me from my perch and closes the door silently behind her. I follow her to the living room.

I clear my throat, but she speaks before I have the chance to. "How was your golf game with Travis this morning?" I suddenly realize I forgot to reply to her text when I got to work after the game.

"Good," I answer quickly. "He shows a lot of determination." Travis only golfed a handful of times before starting our Wednesday morning ritual. Many of our clients have packed schedules, and if you can pitch your financial plan ideas during a round of golf, you are much more likely to get the meeting, which Travis recognizes.

"That's nice," she says, taking a seat on the couch as she moves a baby pillow out of the way. I see her jaw tense, and she might be angry, but I'm not sure.

"I'm sorry I didn't call you after," I state. "Work was a little crazy today." That isn't true. Since being stripped of my main clients, work has been slow. I decide the white lie is acceptable to spare my wife's feelings.

"It's fine. I figured as much. My afternoon meetings

were canceled, so I ended up leaving early and running some errands," she replies.

Making my way around the couch, I sit next to Evelyn. I glance around the living room, silently running through the conversation options I practiced in the car. Our condo is nice, and anyone would consider it quite luxurious as far as the finishes, but its size is a small fraction of what my home with Lizzy was. Evelyn found the condo. She told me she fell in love with it as soon as she saw the listing, and the location was perfect. After living with Lizzy for years in our home, this place still feels foreign. I caught myself telling someone at work last week I needed to get back to Evelyn's place. They gave me a funny look, but I didn't explain. How do I explain that the woman I am married to doesn't yet feel like my wife and that our place does not feel like home?

"Anything exciting happen at work today?" I ask, deciding it best to ease into the conversation.

"Same old thing," she huffs. "Honestly, I'm not sure how much longer I can do this."

My brows stitch together in confusion. "I don't understand, do what?"

"Work at that godforsaken place."

"I'm confused. I thought you loved your job."

"Oh, I do," she quickly interjects. "It's such a depressing place sometimes." I'm surprised by her description.

"I didn't realize you felt that way," I admit. "Is there anything I can do?"

She shakes her head and looks out the window. "I used to be excited about the idea of helping people, but it feels like they make it harder and harder for me to do that."

"They who?" I ask.

"You know, the powers in charge," she grunts, her voice heavy with sarcasm. She turns her head and looks at me. "Babe, is it okay if we don't discuss my work? Being here with you is the only time I get to forget about that place."

"Of course, if that's what you want," I reply, reconsidering if I should bring up the letter I found in her office.

"How about you? How was your day?" She shifts in her seat to refocus her gaze on me.

I shrug because my day isn't what I want to talk about. I want to talk about the letter I saw in her office. "Fine. Just more of the usual."

Neither of us says anything for a couple minutes. "I think it's Madison," she says eventually.

"What's Madison?" I ask.

"Why I find it so hard to go to work anymore," she answers, apparently changing her mind about not discussing the topic.

"I thought you said you wanted to keep your career after she was born."

"That was before she was here," Evelyn says, and I notice her bottom lip quiver. She is not an emotional person, so this is jarring for me.

"You know you don't have to work," I state.

"I know I don't have to," she says defensively. "But I can't imagine being cooped up in this condo all day with a baby."

"All right, now I'm really confused. Which is it? Do you want to stay at home with Madison or go to work?"

Her brown eyes widen into a thoughtful stare. "I don't want to push."

I shake my head. "Push about what?"

She hesitates briefly before she explains, "I want to give Madison the perfect life."

"I do too."

"I don't want her growing up in the city, especially this city."

"So this is about moving? You don't like your job because you want to move. How does that even make sense?"

"Why do you do that?" she hisses.

"Do what?"

"Try to make me sound crazy." Her words strike me as if they have a dagger's edge. Lizzy used to tell me I did the same thing to her. She would share something with me, and I always made her feel like she was crazy.

"I'm sorry, that isn't my intention. I'm trying to understand."

"I want to be home with Madison all the time, but I want it to be in a place where we can enjoy being a family."

"And we can't do that here?" I inquire.

"I told you how hard Boston is for me," she says. "It doesn't help that everyone at work knows I married you and who your ex-wife is."

"Honestly, I was a little surprised to find out you were using my name professionally," I confess.

"I am your wife," she huffs, glaring at me.

"I'm not saying I mind, but don't you think that brings you more attention?"

She shoots me a confused look. "Wait, how do you know I'm using your last name at work?"

"I stopped by your office a couple days ago." I sigh. It looks like now is as good a time as any to find out about the secrets my wife is keeping from me.

"You did? Why didn't you tell me you were there?"

"I wanted to surprise you for lunch, but they told me you were out on a patient evaluation. I guess I should have called ahead. When I stopped by, I saw the name outside your office." She frowns, and I wonder what I said that upset her. "If you don't like the attention my last name brings, it's okay for you to continue using your maiden name professionally. That's all I'm saying."

"I'm excited and proud to be your wife. I shouldn't have to hide it."

"Are you sure?"

"What's that supposed to mean?" she demands.

I should stop the conversation, but my mouth is no longer listening to my brain. "Are you afraid to tell your family about me because of Lizzy and everything that happened?"

"What are you talking about?"

"Look, I want you to know I wasn't snooping." She shifts uncomfortably in her seat as I talk to her. "I was looking for a pen and paper to leave you a note when I found the letter from your dad."

She blinks at me repeatedly but says nothing.

"I'm not mad," I assure her, though part of me is hurt.

"I just want to understand why you lied to me. Why did you tell me he was dead?"

"Well, I'm mad," she snaps. "My father is dead."

"Evelyn, I saw the letter from him, and it was recent," I argue.

"Do you mean my stepfather?" she clarifies, lifting her brows. "I didn't lie to you. My birth father is dead, just like I told you. I can't believe you read my letter."

I shake my head. "I didn't read it," I answer. "I'm sorry, I made an assumption."

"You thought I would lie to you about something like that? What kind of person do you think I am? I can't believe you—"

"I know," I interject and reach out for her, but she pulls away from me. "I'm sorry, I knew there had to be an explanation."

"Why didn't you just ask me when you saw the letter?"

"I don't know . . . because I'm an idiot." The way she's looking at me tells me how desperate I sound.

She stands and crosses her arms as she stares out at the city. I stand as well and approach her cautiously from behind. I reach out and place a single hand on her hip, and relief washes over me when she relaxes her body against mine. I know there's hope for me to fix this. My desire to be completely honest with her causes me to consider telling her about Savannah showing up at my office, but I think better of it. It will only serve to frighten her more, and I'm confident the warning I gave to the girl will have her keeping her distance in the future.

"I'm sorry." Her voice cracks when she speaks, but she doesn't turn to face me.

"What on earth would you ever have to be sorry for? I was the one who jumped to conclusions," I insist.

There is a lingering silence as I wait for her to respond, but she says nothing.

"Can you forgive me?" I ask.

She trembles slightly in my grasp, and when her breath heaves, I realize she's crying. "Ev, what's wrong?"

A whimper comes out as she breaks free from my hold. She pushes past me to flee to our bedroom, but before she can escape, I grab her wrist and pull her back.

"Please," she cries. "I can't. It's too hard."

"What's too hard?" I ask as I guide her back to the couch. Evelyn has always felt stoic to me, so I'm not sure how to process her fragile state.

She collapses onto my shoulder as she proceeds to break down into sobs. Oddly, it's as close as I have felt to her in our entire relationship. Being with someone who never shows their vulnerabilities, especially when they have seen all of yours, can unbalance a relationship.

"There are things you don't know about me," Evelyn admits through her tears.

"I'm sure there are lots of things you don't know about me as well," I say. It is true. She knows about Lizzy and Alison, but there is so much more about me that we have never discussed. I don't like talking about my childhood, so why would I expect her to be different?

She sits upright, wipes her tears away with the sleeves of her shirt, and drags her eyes up to my face. She clears her throat. "Like what?"

Her question takes me by surprise. I didn't think of anything specific when I made the statement. "Huh?" I grunt. "Oh, well, I don't know. I guess I haven't told you a lot about my father either."

"I know he's wealthy," she replies.

"He was also absent and had zero desire to be any regular fixture in my life when I was growing up, but somehow, he still thinks he gets a say in how I live my life."

"I mean, I kind of knew that." She smiles slightly.

I think for a moment of something I haven't shared with her. "On my tenth birthday, I told my mom I wanted my dad at my birthday party more than anything. Don't ask me why. Apparently, I was a kid who liked to torture himself." As I retell the story, there is a pang in my chest, and I'm annoyed it still causes a reaction in me. I sigh, then continue, "My mom spoke to him, and he agreed but had some rules we had to follow. It had to be late at night when he wouldn't be seen sneaking into my mother's place. Nobody else would be allowed to attend except my mother and me. And he would send my mother money so I could buy my gift because he couldn't be seen purchasing a toy for a child. I was so excited. Every day after school, I came home and rearranged my room until I thought it looked perfect. I made sure all my medals and trophies were on prominent display. The big night came, and I sat there waiting with my mom all night, but he never showed. He didn't even call. My mom made excuses for him, but I knew he was teaching me a lesson. He wanted me to know my place in his life, and I wasn't someone who got to make requests like the one I did."

"Nathan, that's awful," Evelyn says as she lifts a hand to my cheek before leaning in and planting a tender kiss on the same spot. I like this side of her. I haven't seen it very often, but I hope to show her she can trust me to show it again.

I shrug. "It's life. I guess, in a way, I'm a stronger person for it."

"I know what you mean," she adds before she shifts and faces forward. I can tell she doesn't want to look at me as she shares her story. "I told you the truth about my dad dying. My mom remarried pretty quickly. I think the idea of being alone scared her." Her shoulders drop a little, and I can see the sadness around her like a blanket. I reach out and start to stroke her back.

"I was glad when they married," she continues. "Mom had been so sad when Daddy died; it was nice to see her happy again. Her new husband seemed nice enough. I found out pretty quickly he wasn't." Her voice shakes.

"You don't have to talk about this if you don't want to," I say.

She shakes her head. "I want you to know. He would come into my room after everyone was asleep and tell me I was special and what a pretty woman I was turning into."

"I'm so sorry," I say, wishing I could take her pain away.

"I thought about telling my high school counselor, but I was worried they would take my sister away from my mom," she explains. "So I decided to tell my mom about what he was doing. She told me he already told her how I tried to seduce him."

I ball my hands into two fists. "That piece of shit."

"I swore to her that I was telling the truth, but she told

me I needed to leave." Evelyn collapses against the back of the couch, the weight of the memory too much for her. "I ended up living with a friend's family until I graduated, and I never looked back."

"How does he know you're here?"

"My sister knows where I am. He convinced her to tell him where I was when they found out my mom has cancer." Her revelation surprises me.

"Wait, your mom's sick?"

She nods.

"I had no idea. Do you need to go see her?"

"I told my sister my mother made her decision when she took my stepfather's side."

"Are you sure? I hate for you to do something you might regret later."

She turns and looks at me. The sadness is gone, and there's something else behind her eyes. Something that makes me shiver. "She made her choice, and I made mine."

"I'm sorry," I offer, unnerved a little by the coldness in her response.

"I won't let him victimize me all over again. I thought you would understand how important it is to protect our little family." She sighs, and I can see her soften as she does.

"I do."

She shrugs.

"Evelyn, I promise, I'll never let anyone hurt you or Madison," I assure her, placing a hand on her leg.

Her eyes connect with mine. "You shouldn't make promises you can't keep."

"How can you say that?" I ask, sounding more defensive than I mean to.

"How do you think Liz is going to handle you having a new family?" she asks pointedly.

"I told you, I will make sure Liz keeps her distance."

"She admitted to planning the murder when she found out Alison was pregnant. She already threatened me when I went to see her in prison. Then you tell me she left a baby rattle at your old house? I don't see how you can promise to protect us when she's clearly unstable, and you're not willing to take any steps to keep us safe."

"She knows better than to come anywhere near our family." I'm confident not telling her about Savannah's visit is the right call. If she's already this upset, I can't imagine what hearing Lizzy's lies about her would do.

"I hope you're right." Just as Evelyn says the words, the baby monitor comes to life with the mutterings of Madison.

"I'll get her," I offer.

Evelyn stands before I can. "No, I'll get her."

I hear her on the monitor a moment later, whispering soothing sounds to our daughter. "Don't worry, baby girl, Mama will keep you safe." The words sting as I can't help thinking she said them because she doesn't trust that I will be able to do that for her. She doesn't realize I will stop at nothing to protect our child.

10

I've lost count of how many times Evelyn has looked at her phone. I reach out and flip it over so that it's face down on the table. She peers up at me, wide-eyed. "What if the sitter calls?"

"Then we'll hear it ring. You don't have to keep looking at it," I assure her. She looks unconvinced. "Ev, we haven't had a date since Madison was born. We need this." The truth is, we need this more than Evelyn can understand. I want to love my wife the way a husband should, but we skipped over the part of our relationship where we got to know each other. If I'm going to be the best husband I can be, I need to figure out how to fall in love with this woman. I don't want to love her only because she gave me my daughter, but because she deserves to be cherished for her. I hope this night will be a step toward finding that connection.

"Candlelight dinners at home are still dates," she replies, looking up at me.

I shake my head and laugh. "I'm not sure I can handle one more cold meal from DoorDash."

She stiffens. "Well, I'm sorry, I'm not the homemaker you want me to be."

"Evelyn, that's not what I meant," I quickly state. "I just think we need a nice evening out for both of us."

She frowns. "Maybe you're not wrong." The bottle of wine we ordered arrives, and I take a sip before giving my approval. We both sit silently while our glasses are filled, and we are once again alone.

Evelyn reaches across the table and scoops up her glass of wine, taking a sip. I smile at her, struggling to find a conversation starter. "How's work?" I ask at last.

She shrugs. "Same as always."

"I know you mentioned the other night that you thought you may want to quit," I press, trying to spark some engagement.

She shrugs again. "I was having a bad day," she says, dismissing my statement.

I tilt my head, confused. "So you don't want to quit?"

"I don't know, maybe. It's not like I can make this decision in an instant," she huffs.

I find it irritating that she always gets defensive when I try to talk with her. I miss how easy things were with Lizzy, at least until Matthew. Ev never seems to laugh. Maybe it's my fault. Perhaps, she can sense I'm only half present most of the time.

"Of course," I reply, shaking my head. "I didn't mean to make you think I was pressuring you."

"I don't."

"So," I start, trying to think of something light to shift

the mood, "funny story, I was in the middle of a meeting at work, and when it was my turn to present, I stood and noticed that as I was talking, everyone in the room seemed to be staring at my crotch."

Evelyn tilts her head, and I can see she's interested in what I'm saying.

"My first thought is I must have left my zipper down, so I casually turn around and try to check as discreetly as I can, knowing everyone is still looking at me, but my zipper is exactly where it should be. I finish my talk while all eyes are still fixated on my nether regions. When I sit back down, I see it," I say and then pause, letting the suspense build.

"What was it?" Evelyn asks.

I offer a tight-lipped grin. "Apparently, Madison had spit up on my pants, and I hadn't noticed, so there was a big white stain right on the crotch. I don't even want to think about what they all thought it was, based on the location." I burst out laughing at the embarrassing moment, but Ev only slightly chuckles.

"I guess you had to be there," I add awkwardly.

Her eyes lock onto something over my shoulder, and her breath catches in her throat. I start to turn my head to see what has caused the reaction when she grabs my hand.

"Nathan, I need to know," she says with an urgency in her voice. "Have you given any more thought to the move?"

The sudden change in topic catches me off guard. "I . . . I mean, well, now that you ask, I have been thinking about it."

She glances over my shoulder again and then back at me. She forces a smile and then grips my hand tighter. "I'm so sorry. I want to have this conversation, but I have to use the restroom. Can you hold that thought?"

"Of course," I answer, standing as she excuses herself. I watch her move toward the back of the restaurant before I sit back down.

After taking another sip of my wine, I catch myself looking at my phone. I slip it into the breast pocket of my jacket and try to refocus my attention on the dinner. She wants to know if I've thought about the move. It's practically all I think about.

If I'm frank with myself, sometimes it feels like I'm married to a stranger. I knew we were rushing things, and a part of me thinks I was in no state back then to be making decisions about marriage, but none of that matters now. I made my choice, and this is my chance to do things better. If nothing else, Madison deserves that.

Moving away from everyone we know isn't the part that scares me. It isn't even leaving my job. What really frightens me is that once we move, Evelyn will be the only person I have in my life. What if, despite my best efforts, I never love her? I can't leave Madison. I am determined to be part of her life. I don't want to be a part-time dad either. I want to be there for all of it, but can you make yourself love someone? Is love even required to have a good marriage?

I think about a conversation I recently had with Travis. Marriage is work, and anyone who tells you differently is lying. Was that what went wrong with Lizzy and me? Were we not putting in the work? My chest aches when I think of Lizzy. I wonder where she is right now, at this very moment. Is she staying at her mom's now that she has been released? Is she getting the help she needs? Does she have a good support system around her? I know her mother can be pretty toxic. I bite my lip, angry that I let my thoughts drift to her. She's not my wife anymore. She's not my concern. She plotted to kill Alison, I remind myself. She threatened Evelyn.

I try to imagine Lizzy threatening anyone, but I can't think of what that would even look like. The truth is, though, before the police uncovered the proof that Lizzy was stalking Alison, I never thought she was capable of that either. Lizzy and I may have loved each other, but our relationship was built on one lie after another. I own my part in how everything happened. Now though, I have a chance to be better with Evelyn and Madison.

Evelyn sits down across from me. Her face is flushed, and her breaths are shallow. I look over my shoulder toward the direction she came from but only see two servers crossing paths. I turn back and look at her, and my brows furrow. "Are you okay?"

"Huh?" She gasps, looking around the restaurant before reconnecting her gaze on me. She shakes her head. "Yeah, I'm fine, but I did call the sitter—"

"Evelyn," I say in a disappointed tone.

"I know, I'm sorry," she offers before continuing. "But I'm glad I did. She said Madison has been fussy, and she can't seem to calm her down."

Evelyn looks around the restaurant again. She seems worried, perhaps even frightened. "Are you sure you're okay?" I ask, glancing around again.

"I'm fine. I would just feel better if we went home."

"We haven't even ordered yet," I reply, frustrated.

"I know. I just don't think I'll be able to enjoy myself knowing that Madison is upset."

Is that what has her so rattled? How can I not take her home when she's trying to be a good mom? There is so much I don't know about Evelyn, but the concern she shows for our child is enough that this is all worth the effort. "Of course," I acquiesce, motioning for the server so I can pay for the wine.

EVELYN DOESN'T SAY much on the way home. She stares out the window, and as usual, I'm left wondering what she's thinking. I consider bringing up the move, telling her I have thought about it, and if it's what she wants, I'm on board. I can tell she's distracted, though, so I decide it's not the best time for this conversation.

I pull into my parking spot, and as I head around to open Evelyn's door, she exits before I have a chance.

"I'm sure everything is fine," I assure her as we approach the elevator.

"Yeah, I'm sure it is." She smiles at me, but I can still see the worry in her eyes.

When we enter the condo, Evelyn heads straight for Madison's room. I walk into the living room and greet the babysitter, who is sitting on the couch consuming some sort of reality television.

"Hi, Whitney," I greet her.

"That was fast," the girl says, looking up at me, still partially engaged in the show she was watching.

I sigh. "When Evelyn found out Madison was being fussy, she wanted to head home."

"Huh . . .?" The girl looks at me with a puzzled stare. "She ate right after you two left, and she's been asleep ever since."

"What?" I ask, trying to make sense of what she's saying.

"Yeah, she's been a total angel," she says as she stands.

"You didn't tell my wife that she was being fussy?"

She shakes her head. "No, I haven't talked to her since you guys left." She lied. Evelyn lied to me. Why would she do that? "Is everything okay, Mr. Foster?"

I force my gaze back to the sitter. "Yeah, Whitney, everything is great. Are you okay if I Venmo you the money?"

She shrugs. "Sure. I guess. Call me if you need me again."

"Will do. Thanks," I say as I walk her to the door.

When I finish locking up, I make my way to Madison's room and stand in the doorway. Evelyn is staring out the window over Madison's crib. I tell myself new mothers worry about their children. The lie was likely innocent, a way for her to exit our evening and get back home to Madison. Despite my reasoning, I can't stop thinking about how the mistruths are adding up. Was Savannah right? Is Evelyn not who she pretends to be?

11

In the distance, construction noises fill the air. I squint, peering out my windshield as Brad exits his Maserati he just parked in his spot next to the entrance of the building. It's hard to imagine I was on track to make partner in the firm a couple of years ago, and now I'm contemplating when to deliver my notice.

I know it's a conversation I need to have with the partners, and some things will need to happen. The clients need to be handled carefully when dealing with the sums of money we do. I also know my father will catch wind of it as soon as I talk to them. He's already furious with me for marrying Evelyn so quickly. He has made it abundantly clear I will not be receiving any additional funds from him to support this family since I did not consult him about the decision. He's used to having power over the people around him, wielding his money like some sort of weapon, but he didn't even come into my thought process when I found out Evelyn was pregnant. After everything that had happened with Lizzy and Alison, all I could think about was doing what was best for that baby.

When my father learned of Evelyn's pregnancy, his words were not gentle. He told me I was a fool and that women like her knew their place, and she would either accept it or be left fending for herself. He wanted me to treat Evelyn like he had my mother. She didn't come from our world, he said. He pointed out that Lizzy hadn't either and was all too happy to note I should pay attention to how that turned out. My father hasn't figured out that I had come to an obvious conclusion through everything that happened to me in recent years. I don't like the world we come from. If I had listened to Lizzy all those years ago when she told me we didn't need his money or his influence, maybe things would have turned out differently.

The moment I give my notice and my father hears, he will apply the pressure. He will try to use everything in his arsenal to show me how much I need him. I have to be ready to cut all ties and say goodbye to every aspect of that life, and while I know it's what I want, it doesn't make it any less scary.

After I'm confident enough time has passed, and Brad is likely in his office, I exit my car and make my way into the building. I keep my head down and avoid eye contact with everyone. With everything on my mind, the last thing I'm interested in is being forced to make small talk.

I see my office straight ahead and sigh a breath of relief that I'm about to make it to my sanctuary without having to speak to a single soul. "Mr. Foster." I hear my name as I near the doors. I turn to see Brad's latest assistant approaching. While I have been on the hunt for an assistant, she has been picking up the slack. I'm embarrassed I can't remember her name. Brad always makes up pet names for his assistants, and at the moment, the only name I can think of is "Bunny." I know it isn't her name, so instead, I decide to avoid names altogether out of respect for her.

"Yes, good morning," I say with a smile, wishing I had been a little stealthier on my journey to my office.

"Someone left this note for you." She smiles at me. I'm relieved she's not here because Brad wants to see me. It's too early for me to tolerate his brand of douchebaggery.

She hands me an envelope with my name on it. I glance at the back, and it's sealed.

"Did you happen to see who left it?" I ask, looking around the office briefly.

She shakes her head. "I'm sorry, I'm not sure who they left it with. Someone dropped it at my desk since I'm sorting your mail until—well, since I'm sorting your mail right now."

"Thank you," I say. "And also, thank you for all the extra work you're doing. I'm working hard to find a replacement for my assistant." That was a lie. I stopped looking when I started thinking about quitting the firm. I was going to do it. I was going to quit, and there would be no need for an assistant. There would be no more Brad, no more late nights at the office, no more taking clients to strip clubs. I used to love my job. It made me feel important and influential. However, after everything I went through in recent years, my opinion has changed.

"It's no problem at all, Mr. Foster," she says.

I enter my office, closing the door behind me. I look at the writing on the envelope again. The way my name is written. It's familiar. My stomach sinks.

I tear open the letter and confirm my suspicions. It's from Lizzy.

I drop the letter onto my desk as if holding it might somehow be dangerous. I can't believe she has the nerve to drop a note off to me. Did she do it, or did she have one of her little prison friends do it? She must have assumed she would be recognized if she came and delivered it herself. What could she possibly want?

Curiosity overwhelms me, and I pick up the letter and peer at the scribbled warning.

Dear Nathan,

Neither of us has given the other much of a reason to trust one another. Despite that, I am asking you to do just that. I hope you can see that I have no reason to lie to you, not anymore. I write to you solely from a place of concern as a woman who used to be your wife. Evelyn is not who you think she is. Be careful. She's dangerous.

-Lizzy

I reread the brief letter. If anything became apparent during the trial, she's right that our marriage lacked any sort of honesty. She isn't asking to see me. She isn't asking me to come back to her. She seems to only warn me. Is it as innocent as that, though, I wonder?

Her motivation could be to ruin my relationship with Evelyn. Evelyn told me Lizzy threatened her when she went to see her in prison. Could this all be part of Liz's plan? Is my ex-wife that manipulative? I was wrong about Lizzy in the past. I never thought she would hide cameras in Alison's house. I never thought she was capable of planning Alison's murder. Was I also wrong, though, when I turned my back on Lizzy? Did I drive her to the state she was in through my affair only to abandon her when she needed me most? A jury overturned her conviction. They decided that the DNA evidence overlooked during the first trial created enough reasonable doubt that she had carried out the murder.

My stomach twists as I think about the crime scene photos the police showed me when they questioned me about Alison's murder. I force the thoughts from my head. Even though a jury found enough reasonable doubt to release her, it doesn't mean she's innocent. As Evelyn pointed out to me, the DNA was from a random person who had zero links to Alison and had been missing for years. There's a chance it was some sort of contamination at the lab. There is still a chance that Lizzy killed Alison, though my gut tells me she didn't.

I crumple up the letter and throw it in the trash can under my desk. I won't let Lizzy destroy my new family. Evelyn may have some secrets, but I know Lizzy's dark side now and what she's capable of. Even if it's not murder, it's still frightening.

12

As a kid, I slept with the light on. I didn't have a father there to keep guard and protect my mother. It was my job as the man of the house, and I would not let anyone hurt my family. As a man, I have the same urges of protection, yet somehow, I was the one who broke my family. I was the one who strayed from Lizzy. I blame her for the things she did, but the truth is, what I did to her put her in the place where she began to let the darkness creep in.

I think about the letter in the trash can under my desk. I haven't been able to stop thinking about it all day, no matter how much I try. I warned Savannah to tell Lizzy she needed to leave me alone. She either didn't take the words back to Lizzy, or my ex wholly disregarded them. I stand and make my way to my car, heading in the direction of home.

Most of the day, I avoided my co-workers and most importantly Brad. While I know some conversation is needed with the partners, I am in no state to have it. If my father reacts the way I assume he will, I need to negotiate the best exit financially for my family and me. Something that will require me to be clear-headed, which I am most certainly not after Lizzy's letter.

When we found out Lizzy was being released from prison, Evelyn begged me to file for a restraining order on her. Considering she plotted to kill a previous girlfriend of mine, it wasn't hard to find a judge to grant the request. She's not allowed to come near any of us. Sending me this letter is a significant risk to herself. All it would take is one phone call from me, and I could have her arrested for violating the order. I can't figure out why she would put herself at such significant risk. Lizzy has to know how angry it makes me that she's trying to undermine my relationship with Evelyn.

Is she determined to create a wedge between Evelyn and me? What could her possible goal be? I'm remarried. It's abundantly clear there is no going back to the way things were. I'm a father now. She knows that, so what could she possibly hope for with her interaction?

The night I met Evelyn, I didn't think much about her. She sat in on a grief group I attended at the local hospital. It's funny, I told Liz she needed to be in counseling after Matthew died, but I hadn't realized how much I also needed it. After losing everyone I cared about, I decided I had nothing left to lose. I didn't speak at the first few meetings, but when I finally did share, it was like I let go of the biggest secret of my life, and I could finally walk upright again.

I assumed Evelyn was attending the meeting, the same as me, but when she reached out later and told me she worked at the hospital, I realized she was there in a more official capacity.

Looking back, it unnerved me a bit when Evelyn showed up at my home. I thought she was one of those crazy trial stalkers. There were plenty. We got to talking, though, and it was like someone finally understood what I was going through.

I wanted to hate Lizzy for what she did to Alison, but more than that, I hated myself for what I did to everyone I claimed to care about. The relationship with Evelyn was entirely accidental. A night of drinking and sharing too many sad stories left us both in a vulnerable place.

I tried to break things off with Evelyn on multiple occasions. After everything I went through, it felt selfish to lead Evelyn on. A relationship was the last thing I needed to be in. Evelyn insisted I was better since my relationship with her started; she was good for me. I couldn't say she was wrong. Her counsel brought me through some pretty dark nights, but a relationship wasn't fair to her since it was one-sided.

As I pull into my parking spot at the condo, a particular memory of when Evelyn told me she thought she might be falling in love with me comes to mind. I told her she didn't know me, but she insisted she could see the real me. The one who was conflicted about all the bad I did and rejected by my father. She saw through all my bullshit. Part of me hoped that if I was with her, I could start to become the man she saw when she looked at me.

Looking back, I know it isn't complicated. I was miserable and lonely. Evelyn filled a void in my life that made me feel normal again. If Madison hadn't come along, I'm confident I would no longer be with her, and maybe that makes me a complete piece of shit human being. But the fact is, our daughter is here, and I will be present as her father.

I make my way upstairs and open the front door. Evelyn stayed home with Madison today. She told me she wasn't feeling well, but I think there's more to it. Maybe it has to do with her recent revelation that she isn't enjoying work anymore. Or perhaps it is all about living in Boston, surrounded by so many reminders of my life with Lizzy. I want to ask her, but I seem to always fail at finding the right words. I walk to the nursery, but Madison is not in her crib. I move to our bedroom, and I see Evelyn asleep with Madison nuzzled against her.

I move in closer, studying Madison's sleeping face. She looks so peaceful. I haven't figured out if any of her features are mine. She doesn't look anything like me. Honestly, she doesn't look like Evelyn either, but to be fair, I have never seen baby pictures of Evelyn. Evelyn keeps telling me that babies don't start resembling their parents until they get older. I'm excited to see which traits of mine she will inherit. The deepest part of me hopes she only takes away the good from me. I inherited my father's worst qualities, and I hate that about myself.

Evelyn stirs and looks up at me. She slips Madison off her arm and sits upright, wiping the sleep from her eyes. Madison stirs a little before falling back to sleep. "I didn't hear you come in," Evelyn whispers.

"I was trying not to wake you," I say.

She shakes her head. "No, we should get up. Madison won't sleep tonight if I let her nap too long."

"Oh, let her sleep a little longer," I plead, peering at our daughter. "She looks so peaceful."

Evelyn furrows her brow. "Is everything okay?" she asks me. Everything isn't okay. Lizzy didn't heed my warning and reached out to me after I explicitly warned her not to, but if I tell Evelyn, she won't handle the information well. What's worse is, if I tell her, she will want me to call the police. I don't wish Lizzy back in prison. I just want her to leave us alone.

I motion to her with my head toward the living room. "Can we talk?"

Standing, she tucks pillows around Madison's body before joining me in the hallway. "What is it?" she whispers.

I sigh. She needs to know where I'm at on things. "I've been thinking about it, and if it's what you want, we can move."

She blinks at me repeatedly, and I can tell she's uncertain she heard me correctly. "Really?"

I nod, and a smile peels across her face as she throws her arms around my neck. "Oh, Nathan."

"Now listen," I warn as she pulls away and plants herself back on the soles of her feet. "It will take some time for me to leave the firm. I'll need to take care of some client hand-offs, but I think you're right. It would be good for our family to start over somewhere else." Somewhere Lizzy isn't.

"That's fine. I'm sure it won't be a quick process for me to leave the hospital either."

"Wherever we end up, I figure I can start a small private practice as a financial advisor. Heck, I might even be able to work from home to be closer to you and Madison."

Evelyn is practically vibrating with excitement, and I wish it was a side of her I saw more. "That sounds perfect."

"I don't want you to think it will be anywhere close to the income we're used to, but between me picking up some clients and the real estate investments I'm liquidating, we'll be comfortable enough," I explain.

"I don't care about the money. You and Madison are all I need," she says as she hugs me again.

I sigh a breath of relief. I have a plan to leave the past behind us finally, and I need to make it happen before Lizzy decides to reach out again. The truth is, now that Lizzy is out, I'm worried less about what she might do and more about why I can't seem to get her out of my mind.

13

The condo's elevator opens, and as Evelyn and I are about to step out, I pause.

"What is it?" she asks.

"I forgot my work badge; I need to go back up," I groan. I'm still not used to needing one to get into the building. They implemented a security feature last month at work to ensure guests check in at the front desk and to avoid unwanted visitors. It didn't prevent Savannah from finding an excuse to be shown into my office, though, so to me, it feels like more of an imposition than a helpful policy.

Evelyn glances at her watch, then back up to me. "We have an all-hands-on-deck meeting this morning."

I shake my head, lean forward, and kiss her on the cheek. "You go ahead. I'm fine."

"Want to have lunch?" she asks, eyes wide.

"Let me check my calendar when I get to work, and I'll text you." She nods and says goodbye before I step back into the elevator. When I go back into the condo, Bridget is already feeding Madison.

"Mr. Foster." I can tell by her voice that I've startled her.

"Hi, Bridget." I smile, letting the door fall closed behind me as I race toward the master bedroom. "Don't mind me. I just forgot something. I'll be gone in a flash."

She continues with her business as I race over to the dresser along the wall on Evelyn's side of the bed. I grab the badge and spin around to leave, but when I do, I accidentally bump Evelyn's nightstand with my leg, causing a picture frame to tumble to the ground. I drop my stuff onto the bed and hold my breath as I bend down to check to see if the glass is broken.

"Is everything okay, Mr. Foster?" I hear Bridget call back to me.

"Yes, just me being clumsy," I reply. I sigh a breath of relief when I pick up the frame and see the glass is intact. I go to return it to Evelyn's nightstand and hear a metallic clang hit the wood. From the corner of my eye, I can see something has fallen onto the top of the nightstand.

I return the frame and pick up the object. It's a key. It must have been wedged behind the backing of the frame. I sit on the edge of our bed, studying it for a moment. The base of the key is plastic, and printed on its side is the name Store-All. I recognize it as a local storage facility chain.

"Mr. Foster?" I hear Bridget's voice getting closer. I shove the key into my pocket, scoop up my belongings from the bed, ensuring I have my badge, and race out of our room. I lift my badge into the air and smile at Bridget, now holding Madison as she stands just outside my bedroom.

"Got it," I say and race out the front door, down the elevator, and to my car.

Why does Evelyn have a key to a storage locker? More importantly, why is she hiding it from me? It was obviously tucked into the picture frame, which means she doesn't want anyone to know about whatever is inside the unit.

I'm being paranoid, but I can't shake the feeling that Evelyn has misled me about a lot more than just her father's death. How many secrets does Evelyn have? She may have technically told the truth about her biological dad being dead, but she never told me about her stepdad. It isn't only the half-truths. She lied to me about the sitter the other night at dinner. She was rattled that night, distracted by something. What if it wasn't because she was worried about Madison? Lizzy was hiding a lot from me. Maybe Evelyn is too.

I just told Evelyn we could move. I'm going to quit my job and leave everyone and everything I know to live with Evelyn and Madison in Michigan because it's what she wants. I need to find out if Evelyn is hiding something before turning my life upside down.

14

"So you are alive?" I hear Brad's voice and look up to see him entering my office.

"Excuse me?" I ask, trying not to sound as annoyed as I am. I shove the storage key I had been playing with only moments before back into my pocket.

"Well, when you missed the strategy meeting this morning, I assumed you must be dead." Brad plops down in the chair across from my desk, rocking it onto its back two legs for a moment.

Last year, Brad went on some sort of wilderness retreat for rich douchebags, and ever since he came back, he always wears the top couple of buttons of his shirt unbuttoned so you can see a hideous necklace with what he claims is the claw of a bear he killed. Nobody believes him, of course, and even if I did, it would only cause me to think less of him, which I find hard to believe is possible.

I shake my head. "Yeah, sorry about that. I forgot my badge and had to head back home to grab it, and by the time I got in, the meeting had already started." I was, in fact, there before the start of the meeting, but since I'm planning on leaving soon, strategizing about new clients seems like something I probably would not be very helpful with.

Brad flexes his fists before grunting. "Oh man, tell me about it. I hate this new security bullshit. I mean, come on, someone breaks in here and tries to shoot up the place, I will end them with just these." He lifts his fists for a moment. "Am I right?"

Brad isn't right, though. I'm almost certain most of his muscles come from steroids, nearly as certain as I am that if there was a real threat in the office, Brad wouldn't hesitate to shove an elderly grandmother out of his way to be the first one out.

"I don't know if they did it because they're worried about someone shooting up the place, or more to make sure only the people who should be here are the ones in the building."

"Are you a partner, Nathan?" Brad asks, and I can tell he's irritated. He doesn't wait for me to reply. "No, I'm a partner. I'm the one in all of the meetings. I might know better than you why they do what they do here."

I grin and nod. "You're right, sorry about that." I'm not sorry. I hate Brad, and I can't wait to give my notice and be done with this place. For a brief second, I consider giving it right then. "Was there something else I can help you with?"

"Yeah, I want to know when you are going to get a new assistant. Bunny has complained that she can't get my work done because of all the extra work she's doing for you." I think he's lying. If I had to guess, Brad's assistant would rather work for me than him and instead used her extra work as an excuse to escape his unwanted advances.

"I have some candidates." I can lie just as well as he can.

The phone on my desk rings, and I'm relieved. "I better get this."

Brad stands up and, placing a hand flat on my desk, leans in and looks into my eyes. "You have one week, and then you can be your own assistant. Got it?"

I nod and pick up the phone, offering a greeting into the receiver as I watch Brad exit, closing my door behind him.

"Hi, Nathan, it's me." I hear Evelyn's voice on the other end.

"Oh, hey, what's up?" My voice cracks, and I start to worry she'll be able to tell I'm hiding something. I'm not ready to tell her I found the storage key she was concealing.

"Is everything okay?"

I assure her I'm fine and ask if she's calling about lunch.

"Actually, no." There's a hesitation when she speaks. "I wanted to ask you a question about Madison."

Panic flutters in my chest. "What about her?"

"Well, I don't want you to think I'm being rude when I ask this . . ." She pauses.

"What's going on, Ev? What are you talking about?"

She sighs. "Do you think you would feel comfortable being on your own with Madison for a couple days?"

"On my own?" I repeat.

"Yeah, as in, do you think you could handle everything if I'm not there?"

"Okay, first of all, I'm her father, so of course, I will be okay." I don't hide my irritation at the question when I respond. "And second, where exactly are you going?"

"Well, when I called a real estate agent in Michigan to tell her to start the search for a place there, it ends up she knows about one that hasn't even gone onto the market yet. She thinks it would be perfect for us."

"A real estate agent?" I blurt out. "Michigan?"

"I know it's fast, but it feels like maybe this is fate."

"Fate? What the hell are you even talking about?"

"Don't talk to me like that!" she exclaims. I suck in a deep breath and try to calm myself.

"I'm sorry, it's just you call me at work and tell me you are heading to Michigan to buy us a house. How did you even find a real estate agent that fast?"

"The real estate agent that helped us find the condo referred me to a branch of theirs in Michigan," Evelyn explains, and I'm left speechless. I haven't even told my bosses I'm planning to leave, and Evelyn is already looking at houses. "I don't understand. Are you mad? You said you were on board with moving."

"I told you I was on board, but I also told you it was going to take me some time to get things in order here at work."

"I know, I'm just going to go look. It doesn't mean we'll buy the place. It's just looking," she insists.

"Evelyn, you didn't tell me you were going to call a real estate agent. If we are going to change everything about our lives, I would like to be part of the process."

"I'm sorry, you're right. I should have talked to you first, but..." She hesitates.

"But what?"

"I already told the real estate agent I could come, and I really want to see this place."

"When are you going?" I ask.

"Later this week."

"There's no way I can take off that soon."

"I know, that's why I was going to go look on my own, and if it's nice, we could go back together."

I think of the storage key I found. Perhaps this is the perfect opportunity to figure out exactly how many secrets Evelyn is hiding from me. "So you're just going to look?" I ask again.

"I promise."

"Okay, Madison and I will be fine," I reply, already thinking about how I'm going to figure out where the storage locker is located.

15

I open the fridge and discover a casserole sitting on the top shelf. Bridget must have prepared it for me while I was at work today. She doesn't say much to me, but she always has a motherly vibe about her. A part of me hopes she will continue being our nanny up until we move. Pulling out the pan, I set it on the stove as the oven heats.

I move around and glance at the baby monitor to ensure Madison is still down for her nap when I feel my phone start to vibrate in my pocket. I pull it out and peer at the screen. Evelyn. I swipe my finger across the phone and lift it to my ear.

"We're fine," I say in a teasing voice.

"Am I that obvious?" she asks.

"It's fine. I know it's hard to be away from Madison," I reply, trying not to reveal that the fact she doesn't seem to trust me to father our kid annoys me.

"Can I talk to her?"

"She's still down for her nap," I reply. "But I can call you when she wakes up."

"Thank you."

"So how was the house?"

"Well, honestly, it was a dud," she answers, and I can hear the disappointment in her voice.

"Oh well, you were just going to look anyway, right?" I remind her, hoping this will put a stop to her constant push to make the move happen immediately. I am on board with the move, but I won't be rushed into the decision about where we are relocating to raise our family.

"Yes, but the real estate agent told me she just got word on a listing she thinks is perfect for us. It's not on the market yet, but she's going to reach out to see if she can get me in to see it before my flight in the morning."

"And how exactly does this real estate agent know about so many properties that aren't listed yet?" I question, the skeptic in me coming out.

"You can be so negative sometimes," Ev grunts. "If you must know, she grew up here, and her dad was the mayor for a while, so she knows everyone," Evelyn explains. "If you give it a chance, you're going to love the town. It's exactly what I pictured in my head when I dreamed about where we would end up." It's becoming evident to me that Ev has been plotting this move for a lot longer than I probably realize.

"Oh yeah?" I try my best to fake excitement.

"I guess we'll see," she says. "Did you get a chance to talk to Brad about leaving?"

"I told you I will," I reply firmly.

"I know. I don't understand why you're waiting. It seems like you would want to get things moving to make sure everything goes smoothly." My face flushes hot. I hate that I need to explain myself in such detail. I take a deep breath and exhale it slowly.

"Can you please trust me to handle things on my end?" I ask.

"You could do it by email if that would make it easier for you," she suggests.

"Damn it, Ev, why can't you ever listen to me?"

"Why are you yelling at me?"

"Because I told you when I agreed to move that this was going to take a little time. Why are you pushing so hard on this?"

"You know I don't want Madison to feel like she's always under a microscope because of who her dad is," Evelyn replies.

"You're being ridiculous. Maddie's a baby. She's not going to remember anything about these years. Why don't you tell me the real reason you are pushing this move so hard?"

She's quiet for a moment, and I briefly wonder if she has hung up, then I hear her voice again.

"Just tell me, am I wasting my time even being here?"

"What?" I ask, confused by her question.

"Do you even plan to quit your job, or were you lying to me about being on board with moving?"

My face is hot, and I feel like I am about to explode with anger. "Are you fucking kidding me right now? It hasn't even been a week since I told you we could move, and your ass is already in Michigan walking through homes, without me, might I add."

"What's that supposed to mean?"

"I don't understand why you have to rush things.

Madison and I could have gone with you if you had been more patient. I feel like you're the one who doesn't want us to be part of your life."

"I can't believe you would say that. How was I supposed to know that the real estate agent would find us something to look at so quickly?"

"You didn't even tell me you had contacted someone."

"I didn't know I needed to."

"I'm just saying this is my life too. I deserve to be included in some of these decisions, don't you think?"

"So now I don't include you in any decisions."

"Oh, my God," I growl in frustration. "Look, I don't want to fight."

"I don't either." Her tone is still sharp.

The oven beeps, so I slide the casserole inside. "Let's talk about this when you get back. You're still coming home tomorrow, right?"

"Yeah, after I look at the other house."

I slam the door to the oven shut and stand, leaning against the counter, trying to relax despite the knots forming in the muscles of my neck.

"I'm sorry," Evelyn whispers, and it sounds like she might cry. I'm not sure whether the emotions are honest or if she's just pretending for sympathy.

"It's fine. We'll figure it out," I answer, trying to soften the tension between us. "Tell me about it."

"Tell you about what?"

"The other house you're going to see," I reply, still irritated about the situation.

"Oh, she didn't say much, except it's been in the

family for over seventy years, and there's certainly going to be a lot of interest."

"So it's an older house?"

"I guess so," she replies. "Is that a deal-breaker for you?"

"Not if it was built well, but maybe I could at least see the town before you commit me to live out my days there."

Evelyn giggles. "I really am sorry. I know I can be pushy."

"That's putting it mildly," I reply, relaxing my stance a little.

"How about I call you on video when I go through it so you can see it?"

"I'd appreciate that," I reply. I was not about to buy a house in a town I had never been to, but if seeing the home with Evelyn helped her understand I was all in on this move, then so be it.

When Evelyn is back, I will sit her down and explain that we need to take our time. We have to make the right choices. Picking the town we'll raise our family in is not a tiny thing. But that isn't the only reason I need the process to slow down. It's clear my wife has some secrets she doesn't want me to know about. I need time to figure out what else she's hiding from me.

"I love you," she says.

"I love you too," I answer back, wishing I meant the words in the same way she did. "I'll call you when Madison wakes up from her nap."

"Thank you."

16

I'm tired. Evelyn usually tends to Madison during the night. I'm a heavy sleeper and don't usually hear her when she gets up, and Ev never wants to wake me, despite my repeated requests. With her out of town, the nighttime feedings have been all mine, and I'm more appreciative this morning. She never complains about a lack of sleep. I'm grateful I have this experience because I'm finding something new to admire about Evelyn. I also can't help feeling a pang of guilt about how stern I was with her on the phone. The fact remains, though, I'm not moving Maddie away from here until I know what else Evelyn is hiding from me.

I watch Madison swatting at the mobile above her head on the play mat. She giggles as a few saliva bubbles escape out of the corner of her mouth. I glance at my phone again, checking the time. Based on the text I received from Evelyn earlier in the morning, she should be at the house with the real estate agent already. I take a sip of coffee and text Evelyn in case she is too distracted to remember.

Nathan: Do you want me to FaceTime you or you me?

My phone rings a moment later, and I answer the video call. Evelyn is smiling at me.

"Sorry, babe," she chimes. "I forgot to call you."

She would be annoyed if the reverse had occurred, but I push the thought from my mind as it will just lead to another argument. "It's fine."

"Hello, Mr. Foster, I'm Beverly Hendricks, and I am so happy to be working with you and your lovely family," a woman's voice off-screen says. Evelyn flips the camera around and turns it in the direction of a middle-aged woman in a pale pink tweed suit jacket with salt-and-pepper hair tucked behind her ears. She looks exactly what I would imagine a small-town real estate agent would look like, and nothing like the ones I'm used to dealing with here in Boston.

"Hello," I reply before I take another sip of coffee.

As the real estate agent describes the home, I listen, and Evelyn moves the camera around the property. It's a Victorian farmhouse with seven bedrooms and seven bathrooms and impressive woodwork. She explains that it has been run as a bed and breakfast for the past fifty years and that many clients come back year after year for regular vacations.

"That's perfect!" Evelyn exclaims, and I'm confused by her response.

"Wait, what?" I ask, but nobody seems to hear me.

"The kitchen is well equipped to handle the guests you would receive, and they are willing to part with all of the furniture, so it is a turnkey opportunity," the real estate agent continues.

"Wait a second, what are you saying? A bed and breakfast?" I question louder now.

Beverly blinks at the camera in confusion a few times. "Well, yes, Mr. Foster, your wife was very clear that you were looking for an income-generating property."

"What? No, that's not right. There has been some sort of misunderstanding."

"Nathan." I hear Evelyn's voice. "Can we talk about this after the tour?"

I'm dumbfounded. "Evelyn, I don't want to raise Madison in a bed and breakfast."

"We can talk about this after," she says to Beverly, motioning for her to continue.

"No, I'm serious," I state firmly. "There is no way we are buying a bed and breakfast, Evelyn."

"Will you excuse me?" Evelyn chimes in a sweet tone as she flips the camera back around and steps out onto the front porch. When we are alone, she looks with a narrow gaze at the camera. Her jaw is tight. "Nathan, you're embarrassing me."

"I don't mean to embarrass you, but don't you think a major life decision like running a bed and breakfast is something we should have talked about in advance?"

"Why? You don't talk to me about decisions you make," she snaps.

"What decisions don't I talk to you about?"

"You just decide you're not ready to tell your bosses that you're leaving, and I'm supposed to be okay with it and wait until you're good and ready?"

"You have lost your mind," I snap.

"I can't do this here," she huffs, and before I can say another word, she ends the call. I try to call her back, but it goes immediately to voicemail. I haven't seen this short-tempered and rash side of her before.

Panic wells inside me. She's my wife, every irrational and controlling bit of her. I'm growing angrier and angrier each time she sends my call to voicemail. I toss the phone onto the couch next to me in frustration.

"Damn it," I mutter when my attention quickly shifts to Madison, still entranced by the stuffed toys dangling over her head. When I get down on the floor next to her, I can almost instantly feel myself relax. She is worth all of this. She's why.

After some time passes, I hear my phone buzz, and I retrieve it from the couch as I head into the kitchen to warm Madison's bottle. It's a text from Evelyn.

Evelyn: I can't believe you embarrassed me like that.

Nathan: I can't believe you're trying to bulldoze me into buying a bed and breakfast.

Evelyn: I am not bulldozing you.

Nathan: Well, what would you call it?

Evelyn: I thought you wanted me to be happy.

Nathan: I do, but that doesn't mean you just get to decide we are moving to a B&B.

Nathan: What were you even thinking?

Evelyn: I don't appreciate the way you're talking to me.

Nathan: And I don't appreciate being blindsided like that.

Evelyn: I told you I wanted to be home with Madison more.

Nathan: You don't have to run a B&B to stay home with our daughter. I'll take care of us.

Evelyn: I am not Liz.

WHEN I READ THE TEXT, I feel an ache in my stomach. She certainly is not Lizzy. Lizzy did a lot of terrible things during our marriage. I'm not naïve as to how utterly broken we were. But Liz wouldn't pull the shit Evelyn is. Lizzy isn't my wife anymore, I remind myself silently. Evelyn is, and if I don't figure out a way to make this work, I might lose Maddie.

NATHAN: What's that supposed to mean?

Evelyn: I don't want you to take care of me. I want to take care of myself.

Nathan: We're supposed to be a team.

Evelyn: Why can't you understand I need something of my own. I won't just be a wife waiting for her husband to come home.

Nathan: You wouldn't be.

Evelyn: I don't want to talk about this anymore.

Nathan: I think we should.

Evelyn: I moved my flight to tomorrow morning.

Nathan: What? Why?

Evelyn: The real estate agent plans to show me a few more houses.

Nathan: Are they houses or something else?

Evelyn: Please stop.

Nathan: Stop what? You're the one who sprang the B&B on me.

Evelyn: I'll be home tomorrow morning.

I STARE at the conversation on my screen, reading and rereading the words. The longer I'm married to Evelyn, the more evident it is that she's a stranger to me. I want to be a good husband and father, but how do I do that when I have zero ideas about how to even communicate with the woman I married? What's worse, how do I do that when I wonder if I can trust her?

I bring the bottle into the living room, and setting my phone down next to me, I scoop Madison up and start feeding her. I look at her eyes and the way her small lips pucker around the nipple of the bottle. My eyes grow wet, and all I can think is how perfect she is.

Is it me? Am I the problem in our marriage? Is Evelyn asking for too much? I have zero desire to be surrounded by strangers day in and day out at a B&B. I want to protect my family and be a good father. How can I do that when so many unknowns surround me? A killer could be staying under our roof, and I would have no idea.

The thought settles over me. A killer could be under our roof. I didn't know Liz was stalking Alison. If I didn't know what my own wife could do, how can I be trusted to protect my family from strangers I know even less about?

Eventually, my mind drifts to the key I found inside the frame next to our bed. Is there nothing in that storage locker except Christmas decorations and old memorabilia from college? My chest tightens as I ponder what else Evelyn could be hiding. Am I being irrational? If I continue to accuse her of things, how long will it be before she decides she's tired of being with a man who doesn't trust her?

Why would she hide it, though? If there's nothing of concern in there, why keep the key in a place so secretive? I need to know what Evelyn's hiding, not just for my sake but for the sake of our family.

17

I stare at the key in the palm of my hand. What would Evelyn say if she found out I had it? Was she trying to hide it? I can't imagine someone keeping a key inside a picture frame if they aren't trying to hide something. I could ask her about it, I think. That would be an open and honest thing for a husband to do. The problem is I have zero clue how Evelyn would react. My gut says she would be furious and accuse me of once again not trusting her, or she would lie. After all, she lied to me before.

I need to know.

If I find out she's not hiding anything from me, maybe I can finally put all of my suspicions to rest and move forward with my family. What the hell is she hiding in that locker? How do I figure out which locker is hers?

I head into the home office and open the drawers, flipping through all the paperwork I can find. Most of it is stuff I brought from my office in my house with Lizzy. What little that belongs to Evelyn does not appear to have anything to do with the storage facility. I consider her office at the hospital, but I'm not sure how I would explain why I was there if someone from her work told her they saw me.

I stare at the name on the key, Store-All. I flip through my phone, find the main number, and dial it.

"Store-All, where all your storage needs are fulfilled, can I help you?" a cheerful voice answers on the other end of the phone.

"Umm . . . yes, hello. I have a problem, and I wondered if you could help me."

"Yes, sir, what can I do for you today?"

I wish I had thought things out more before I called. "Well, you see, my aunt recently died, and well, we are here cleaning out her apartment, and we came across this storage locker key. We searched her entire apartment for any paperwork that might indicate the location of the locker, and we can't find anything."

"I'm so sorry for your loss," the voice says.

"Thank you," I continue. "What I was wondering is if there is any way you could look up and see which locker belongs to her?"

Relief washes over me when the voice says, "Of course, sir, that's something I can definitely help you with."

"Thank you. You don't know what a—"

The voice on the other end of the line interrupts me, and my relief quickly disappears. "All we need to give you that information is the executor of the will who has power over the estate to bring in proof they have that power, the key, and a death certificate."

"What? Seriously? There's no other way? I just need to know which locker is hers."

"I'm sorry, sir, it's company policy."

"Thank you," I say before hanging up the phone. Finding out what secrets Evelyn might be hiding won't be as easy as I thought.

18

A tiny voice in my head keeps telling me that if I'm not willing to ask Evelyn about the storage locker, I should just put the key back where I found it. At one point, I found myself holding the key, standing in front of the picture frame, but then my mind went back to the fact I missed the signs in my last marriage.

I stare at the glass of wine I poured myself an hour ago but haven't touched. My past mistakes have been waging war on my thoughts. I cheated on Lizzy. The one thing I thought I would never do, I did. I had an affair. More than that, I had a relationship with another woman. Alison wasn't just some one-night stand. She became a part of my life. I always wondered what my father told his wife about my mother. Did she know about her? Did she know about me? Was it an arrangement that nobody spoke of but everyone simply accepted?

When my affair started, I convinced myself I would end it eventually. I told myself I needed Alison while

Lizzy and I worked through a rough patch. I knew I was full of shit, but it was easier to pretend.

I convinced myself that I was doing Lizzy a favor by hiding the affair from her. I was such an idiot because I didn't hide anything. She knew all about Alison. She followed us on dates, followed Alison to her house, hid cameras inside her home. When I came home and looked at my wife's face each night, I worried she could see my deceit, but I was so consumed with myself I missed what was right in front of me. She was the one with secrets.

I had no idea what was happening in my own home. If I didn't suspect a thing in my first marriage, wouldn't it stand to reason I should be even more concerned now that I have suspicions about Evelyn? The problem is, I can't figure out whether my mistrust of my new wife was birthed from what happened in my first marriage or if it's merited.

The one fact I keep coming back to: the equation has changed. Protecting Madison is my priority. If Evelyn is hiding something, I have to find out.

I place Madison in the car and drive to the Store-All facility closest to our condo. I have no idea when or where Evelyn rented from, but I feel like I have to try something.

Pulling up to the main entrance, I get out and retrieve Madison's car seat from the back of my car and head toward the door. She's staring at me wide-eyed, and I'm thankful she's too young to understand what her dad is doing. I immediately catch sight of a young woman sitting at the front desk when I open the door. Nobody else is in the office, but I spy a security camera in the top-right rear corner of the room.

"Hello," I offer with raised eyebrows.

"Hi, how can I help you tonight?" I would be shocked if the girl was over twenty, and all I can think is there is no way I would ever want Madison to work alone like that girl is.

I hesitate. "Well, this is kind of embarrassing." She doesn't react. I'd thought about my story all the way here, practicing different responses I might have as I drove. "You see, we are getting ready for a big move out of state, and my wife is out of town looking for our future house." I decide sticking as close to the truth as possible is probably my best bet for believability.

"Okay." She seems confused by the direction of my story.

"Well, you see, while we were packing everything up, I may have accidentally packed my daughter's favorite blanket." I am so good at lying it alarms me. "She can't sleep without it. When I realized what I had done, I went to look for it, and that's when I discovered I had packed it in one of the boxes the movers took to the storage facility."

"Sir, we have twenty-four-seven access to the storage lockers. You're welcome to go and look for your daughter's blanket."

"That's just it. I have no idea which storage locker is ours."

She furrows her brow, and I can tell I'm starting to lose her.

"You see, my wife handled everything. All the paperwork that has the unit information is packed up as well. I tried calling, but she isn't picking up. I don't know what to do."

The girl shakes her head. "I'm sorry, sir, I don't understand what you're asking me to do."

I pull out the key and place it on the counter before I rock Madison's carrier to make sure the woman's attention is drawn to her. "I have the key. If you can, just look up which storage locker it is."

"Oh sure, no problem." She smiles. "Is it in your name?" she asks, shifting the keyboard in front of her.

"No, it would be in my wife's," I reply, trying to act casually.

The girl looks over her shoulder as if she is concerned someone is watching her. "I'm sorry, we're only supposed to give that information out to the account holder."

I rock Madison a little more vigorously. "I'm so relieved that my wife chose a place with such excellent security. It does give me a bit more peace of mind during this stressful move. Well, look, I don't want to get you in any trouble, so I guess I'll keep trying my wife and hope that she eventually picks up. Have a good night," I say, shoving the key back into my pocket and fumbling with the car seat. "I'm so sorry, sweetie. Daddy tried," I whisper to Madison, loud enough for the girl to hear.

I can see the girl shifting anxiously from the corner of my eye. "Wait," she starts as I turn toward the exit, and I can feel my chest begin to swell with excitement. "I mean, I guess since she's your wife and you have the key, there's no harm in giving you the information."

"Oh my goodness, would you do that for me?" I ask,

acting extra excited. "Did you hear that, baby girl? This nice woman is going to help us get your blankie."

"What's your wife's name?" She's smiling, and I feel a slight twinge of guilt using Madison in my scam. It's for her, I remind myself. To make sure she is safe.

I pause and think about the girl's question. When did Evelyn get the locker? Were we already married? Would it be under our married name, or would it have been under her previous name? I take a stab in the dark and hope for the best. "Evelyn Powell."

The girl clicks away at her keyboard. "Hmm . . ."

"What is it?" I ask, assuming I must have gotten the name wrong.

"You're sure she rented it at this location?" she asks.

"Oh my God, I didn't even think about the fact that you all have multiple locations. I know about this one because I drive by it on the way to work." I'm confident she thinks I'm a complete moron.

She continues clicking away until she says, "No problem, but it looks like she is in the Beaumont Avenue location."

Beaumont Avenue. I know the exact location she's talking about because it's near Alison's old home.

The girl scribbles down the locker number on a piece of paper and slides it over to me. "I hope you find your blanket, sweetie," she says to Madison in a high-pitched, soft voice.

I wave the piece of paper in the air as I move toward the exit with Madison's carrier gripped tightly in my other hand. "Thank you. You have no idea how much you just saved me."

"Good luck," she calls after me as I race to the car and secure Madison's carrier into the base of the car seat. I stare at the piece of paper. Beaumont Avenue location. Once I do this, once I invade Evelyn's privacy, I can't undo it. I pull out of the parking lot and head in the direction of our condo. I can stop it right here. I don't have to go any further with this.

Beaumont Avenue . . . I can't stop wondering why she would rent a unit so far away from her old apartment or the hospital. Store-Alls were located all over the city. There had to be a more convenient location for her.

I pull into my parking spot and head up the elevator with Madison, and I'm unlocking the front door when I feel my phone start to buzz. I assume it's most likely Evelyn and race inside, placing Madison's carrier down in the entry, hastily whipping my phone out of my pocket, and answering it without looking at the caller ID.

"Hey," I say, trying to catch my breath, waiting to hear Evelyn's voice on the other end.

"Nathan?" It isn't Evelyn's voice, but I recognize it.

"Emily?" I say, thinking I must be mistaken.

"Are you okay? You sound like you're out of breath."

"I was carrying the baby in," I say.

"Right," she grunts. "The baby." Since college, Emily has been Lizzy's best friend, so her reaction to Madison isn't surprising.

"Why are you calling me?" I ask. "You shouldn't be calling me."

"Trust me, the last thing I want to do is talk to you. I told Liz to call you herself," she replies. "But she said that you wouldn't speak to her."

"She's right. I wouldn't," I reply, but I have my doubts. I'm not sure I could resist talking to her.

"Is Evelyn there with you?" Emily asks.

"That's none of your business," I snap.

Emily is quiet on the other end for a minute.

"Hello?" I question to see if she's still there.

"Well, if she is, it's not safe for you to have this conversation in front of her," Emily continues.

"I'm not going to do this," I warn her as I bend over and lift Madison from her carrier. Making my way down the hall, I take a seat on the couch and tuck Madison under my arm next to me. "I won't let Lizzy drag me into her delusions."

"Will you stop and listen for a minute? You at least owe my friend that much after what you put her through." I hate that she's right about the pain I put Lizzy through.

"Fine. Say what you have to say, then I don't want to hear from you again," I snap.

Emily huffs on the other end of the line. "I told Lizzy she should just let that crazy-ass bitch have you, but she's so damn worried about you and your kid."

"What do you want, Emily?"

She sighs. "I've tracked down Evelyn's parents, and I'm heading to Georgia to talk to them."

"You're what?" I can't believe what I'm hearing.

"Don't worry. They have no idea I know you or Liz. I told them I was doing a story that involved their daughter."

"Are you insane? You can't do that."

"I know you don't believe Lizzy, but I do. That woman you're married to told her that she killed Alison."

"Lizzy's sick, Em. You going along with her delusions isn't doing her any favors."

"She's got some shit she's working through, no thanks to you. But she's not lying about that woman, and I'm going to prove it."

"You don't understand. You can't go talk to her parents," I warn, thinking of the horrors Evelyn shared with me about her stepfather.

"If she's exactly who she says she is, then what are you so worried about?"

"You don't know everything," I plead.

"Then enlighten me," she huffs.

"I can't," I say, not wanting to betray Evelyn's confidence.

"Then I'm going to Georgia," she exclaims.

"Damn it!" I snap, desperate to stop Emily from blowing our lives up. "You don't know everything."

"If you can't give me a good reason why I shouldn't go, I'm going."

I sigh. I don't have any other choice, so I have to tell her. "That's not even Evelyn's real dad. Her real dad died, and that's her stepdad."

"What are you talking about?"

"Not that it's any of your business, but clearly, if I don't tell you, you will end up doing something stupid. Evelyn told me that she cut off all contact with her parents because her stepdad was abusive, and her mom knew and refused to believe her. You have no idea what you're doing by talking to them," I explain.

"Nathan, that's not true," Emily gasps.

"What? Of course, it is."

"I spoke to them over the phone, and her dad was telling a story about when she was a baby. She has a younger sister, so there is no way her stepdad was in her life when she was an infant. He is not her stepdad. She's lying to you."

"What? No, why would she lie about that? That makes no sense."

"I don't know. He said Evelyn was so excited about moving to Boston, but then something changed, and she completely shut them out of her life."

"It doesn't make any sense why she would lie about her dad being dead," I argue.

"Sure it does if she's batshit crazy. Now can you see she's not who you think she is?"

"You're lying," I insist.

"Why would I lie? I don't give a shit who you're with. For all I care, she can stuff you and keep you in the corner."

"Why are you letting Liz drag you into this? She's not going to turn me against Evelyn."

"Seriously? Do you think that's what this is about? I would never help Liz get you back. You're the person who destroyed her life." I want to scream that she's wrong, but I know she isn't. "I'm helping Liz clear her name. It doesn't matter that there is other DNA evidence or that she got released from prison. Until the actual killer is brought to justice, Liz will never be able to get her life back. People will always wonder if she actually did it."

"Fine, so you're doing this to help Liz." I'm not willing

to admit it to Emily, but a part of me is relieved Lizzy has people who care about her the way Emily obviously does. I know better than anyone the way your past can follow you. I can't imagine what it is like for Liz, always suspected by everyone you meet that you might be a killer. "But that still doesn't explain to me why the hell Evelyn would lie to me? It just doesn't make sense."

"I spoke to her parents myself, and they obviously are very distraught over what has happened to their relationship with their daughter. I don't know what she's hiding, but I plan to find out," Emily says.

The letter from Evelyn's father pops into my mind. Did she lie to me? Why? What was Evelyn trying to hide from me? What else is she hiding? I need to see what's inside that storage locker more now than ever.

"Nathan?" Emily's voice breaks through my thoughts.

"I don't think it's a good idea for you to go talk to her family."

"I'm going," Emily confirms. "Liz just wanted to make sure you have a heads-up because if Evelyn finds out we are looking into her, it could mean you and the baby are in danger. Goodbye."

Emily is gone. My mind is racing. Is Emily working with Liz? Are they trying to undermine my trust in my wife? I believe she would never want to help Lizzy get me back. Is this all some plot for revenge because of my affair with Alison? Madison's hand tightens around my finger, and my attention shifts.

"Hey, you," I say, smiling at my daughter as she looks up at me. It's time for me to figure out exactly what her mother is keeping from me.

19

I turn down Beaumont Avenue, my wipers moving back and forth in rhythm as I pull into the parking lot of the storage facility. I retrieve my phone and text the sitter, a knot of guilt forming in my stomach about leaving Madison with Whitney while I go to spy on her mother. Am I so different from Lizzy? Is what I'm doing any better than what she did when she spied on Alison?

I force the thought from my head when I get a reply from Whitney that everything is great. This isn't the same. I'm not doing this from a place of jealousy or just for myself.

Escaping the rain as quickly as possible, I dart through the facility door on my right and start searching the numbers over the locker doors. I go down one hall and turn in another direction, winding through the building until I finally find it. I stand in front of the gate to the storage locker, gripping the key tightly in my hand.

Once I open it, there is no going back. It's just like the letter in Evelyn's office from her father. I resisted opening it because I knew it would be an invasion of privacy, but maybe I should have opened it. Who lies about their father being dead? Even worse, why would someone make up a story about being abused? Evelyn is lying to me, and I need to know what other secrets she's keeping from me.

I slip the key into the lock. I have to do this. I need to put my suspicions to rest. I'll go in, see there is nothing out of the ordinary, then put all this doubt behind me and focus on being the husband Evelyn deserves.

Sliding the gate up, I pull on the cord to the overhead light and step inside. I look around to find dozens of boxes. Some are open, and some are sealed shut. I glance at the sides of the boxes for any writing, but none are labeled. In the back-right corner, I recognize some small furniture items from Evelyn's apartment while we were dating. I rummage through the first open box on my left and find an old alarm clock and some medical journals.

I immediately feel ridiculous. I paid a babysitter to watch our daughter so I could come and sort through all my wife's junk. Relief settles over me as all I see is item after item of everyday household goods in each container. This is it. This is the verification I need that, while Evelyn might have some secrets, she isn't the monster Lizzy wants me to see her as. She isn't hiding anything in this locker. I can lock the gate, put the key back, and go on with my life.

I turn to leave, and as I do, my leg catches on one of the boxes. I freeze, careful not to disturb anything. Just as the box is about to tip over the rest of the way, I lunge for it, catching it just in time to stop the contents from spilling out.

"Damn it," I mutter as I sigh a breath of relief. Holding the rescued box in my hand, I notice something on the top that captures my attention. Placing the box back onto its previous resting spot, I reach in and pull out the large round shape. I study the rubbery texture for a moment, then I realize it's a prosthetic pregnant stomach. As my hand grazes over the cool surface, I'm impressed with how lifelike it is—not only in the way it looks but also in the way the stomach feels. A memory of Lizzy's pregnant curves pops into my mind, and I just as quickly force it back out.

Why would Evelyn have this? Perhaps, she uses it with her patients as some sort of therapy for women dealing with the loss of a child. That must be it, I tell myself, moving the stomach to the side, revealing a shoebox under it. I take a seat on the floor and place the box in my lap, pulling off the lid. I decide I've already come too far. It's not like I am betraying Evelyn more if I continue to look. Maybe I will learn something about her to help me connect better with her.

The box contains pictures of a younger Evelyn. She looks nothing like she does now. Her hair is lighter. I never knew she colored her hair. I wonder which is her natural shade. She dresses differently now than she did in the photos. I look at the images and wonder who the other people are in them. Are they family members, friends, old colleagues? There's so little I actually know about my wife.

I set the pictures aside and dig deeper into the box.

There is a stack of newspaper clippings, and I read the first headline: "Patient Missing After Massive Fire at Psychiatric Hospital." The clipping is from a Georgia newspaper. How was Evelyn connected to that fire? I look at the date of the story. It was right around the time she moved to Boston. Had she worked at that hospital? Is that why she decided to move here? Is that the secret she has been so desperate to keep from me?

I flip through the clippings and see they are all about the fire. There must be something significant about the fire for Evelyn to have all of these. I read through one of the articles, searching for clues. Evelyn's name is there. It says her patient was the one who went missing. I assume that must be why she never told me. I thought she was struggling with my past all this time, but she has her own demons. She's clearly carrying some sort of guilt about the missing patient. I read on; the article says Evelyn was unavailable for comment. I flip to another article and skim it, finding similar details until a chill runs down my spine as I read the name, Patty Dane.

I recognize the name immediately. The DNA found on the weapon that killed Alison was Patty Dane's. The DNA evidence that freed Lizzy from prison. During Lizzy's retrial, it came out that Patty Dane was a patient at a psychiatric hospital in Georgia and had been missing for some time. I reread the article, looking for a detail I may have missed.

I'd had conversations with Evelyn during Lizzy's second trial about the evidence. She never told me she knew Patty Dane, let alone that she had been her doctor.

She had every opportunity to say something about her connection.

It doesn't make sense. I met Evelyn at a grief meeting, but there is no way it's a coincidence that one of Evelyn's patients murdered Alison. My heart is pounding in my ears, and I can feel my palms start to sweat. What does it mean?

I'm now frantically searching through the box of articles. "Killer Wife," "Murderous Matrimony," "Love Triangle Leads to Murder," article after article is about Alison and Liz. Why does Evelyn have these? She acted like she didn't know anything about Liz or me or the trial when I met her. Who am I married to?

I start to search for more clues when I feel my phone buzz. I pull my phone out, expecting it might be the sitter, but my breath catches in my throat when I see it's Evelyn. I consider sending it to voicemail, but I don't want to alarm her. I try to steady my breathing for a moment before I slide my finger across the phone and lift it to my ear.

"Hi, sweetie." My voice cracks slightly, and I wonder if she notices.

"Hi," she says before following it up with a long silence.

"Hey, you still there?" I ask, trying to sound upbeat.

"Yeah," she says in an almost whisper.

"You okay?" I ask.

"What are you doing?" She asks the question, and it almost feels like an accusation is behind her words. I tell myself I'm being paranoid.

"I had Whitney watch the baby so I could run to the

store and pick up a few things. What are you doing?" As quietly as I can, I start to place the items back into the box, doing my best to remember exactly how I had found everything.

"I felt bad about our fight," she says at last.

"Me too," I say, looking around the room, hoping I haven't missed any details. I can't leave until I'm off the phone with her. She'll hear if I pull the gate closed. I stand, frozen, trying to make sense silently in my head of everything I've just seen. "You'll be home tomorrow, though, then we can talk about it."

"Nathan," Evelyn starts but then allows a long silence to linger between us.

"Yes?" I say, holding my breath.

"Are we okay?" Her question catches me off guard.

We are so far from okay, but I can't tell her that. I have to figure out what Evelyn knew about Alison and if she had any involvement in or knowledge about her murder. I need proof, though. I can't risk her taking Madison and me never getting to see her again.

"Of course we're okay. Why would you ask that?"

"You were so upset about the bed and breakfast," she says.

I swallow hard. I need to come across as usual. What would I have said to Evelyn before I found out she lied to me from the moment I met her? "I definitely felt blindsided."

"That wasn't my intention. I've been on my own my entire life. It's hard for me to remember that I'm not making decisions for just me anymore."

"That's understandable." I feel like I will betray myself

and reveal what I've discovered about her at any moment. "Hey, we are completely fine, okay? But I need to check out and get back home to Madison. Is it okay if we talk about this when you get home tomorrow?"

"Oh . . ." She pauses. "Yeah, of course. How's Madison been?"

"As perfect as ever," I say, thinking about how all I want in the world is to be at home, looking at my daughter, making sure she is safe.

"Good. I guess I'll see you in the morning then?"

"I can't wait." I start to hang up when I hear Evelyn speak.

"I love you."

I'm frozen for a moment. I need to say it back, but all I can think is that I have no idea who I'm saying it to. "I love you too," I manage before I hang up the phone.

I pull the cord to the light, close the gate, and lock it up before shoving the key into my pocket. I leave and pull into the grocery store parking lot down the street. I can't risk Evelyn catching me in a lie since it will only make her more suspicious of me, so I grab some diapers and extra formula, despite knowing we have plenty at home, and check out.

Evelyn will be home tomorrow. I have until then to figure out what I'm going to do with the information I've learned.

20

I stare at the clock on the wall. Evelyn's early morning flight should have landed thirty minutes ago. That means she'll be home at any moment. She didn't call or text that she landed safely, but that's not the way Evelyn works. I've learned that much about her during our marriage. It always surprises me how poor she is at communication, even though she's a therapist, but I'm not much better. Perhaps if I were better at it, I would have figured out Evelyn isn't who she said she is long before now.

I barely slept, my mind running through all the things that don't make sense. I considered jotting everything down, but I can't risk her finding it.

Since it's a workday, I finish getting ready. Bridget will be here soon, and I need everything to appear normal. I hear the key in the lock and wonder if it's Evelyn or Bridget. I glance in the mirror, hoping it's not apparent that I haven't slept.

I hear the roller wheels of a suitcase in the hallway.

It's Evelyn. My stomach does a flip as I move into the hallway with a smile and go in for a kiss, wondering if she can see right through me.

"Welcome home," I say, though I feel sick when I see her. I wonder if anything she has ever said to me is the truth.

"Thanks." I can feel her eyes studying me as I move around the place. "Where are you going?" she asks me.

I stop and look at her, forcing a chuckle. "It's a workday. Bridget will be here soon."

She shakes her head as she moves farther into our home, leaving her suitcase near the door. "I told her she didn't have to come today."

I stop and turn my head in her direction, dread welling inside me. "Why would you do that?"

"I missed Madison." She seems annoyed by my question. "If it's okay with you, I called in sick so that I can spend the day with her."

"Oh," I grunt. "I mean, of course, it is. I just thought you would have a lot to take care of, getting ready for our big move and all."

I don't like the idea of her being here alone with Madison. I should feel fine. She has been with her countless times up until now. Evelyn is a great mother, despite being one of the most deceptive people I've ever met.

"Weren't you the one who told me we needed to slow things down?" she asks.

"Well, yes, but I assumed that went in one ear and out the other." I attempt the joke lightheartedly, but from the look on her face, I'm starting to worry that she knows I suspect she lied to me all along. I silently tell myself to stay calm.

"Funny." She smirks. "But seriously, I thought we were going to talk about the B&B when I got home," she says as she follows me around while I finish collecting items for my briefcase.

I pause and turn to look at her. "Well, yeah." I smile. "But I didn't mean the moment you got home. I have meetings today, hon. I'm sorry."

She looks at me, and I can see the suspicion in her eyes. I kiss her on the forehead. "I promise, as soon as I get home tonight, I'll set aside the entire evening to discuss the idea, okay?" I wonder if I'm too agreeable when I speak about the B&B. I was furious over it, and here I am, kissing her on the forehead as I touch on the subject.

She agrees and moves into Madison's room. Instinctively, panic washes over me. I focus on slowing my breathing. I can't let Evelyn think anything is wrong. I need to figure out precisely what she knew and when before doing anything. She lied to me, I know that much, but I need to piece together which parts she lied about.

I stand in the doorway and watch as Evelyn peers down at Madison. There is a tenderness in the way she looks at her. She would never hurt her. I can see that. I hope after some digging, my assumptions about Evelyn are wrong, and there's a reasonable explanation for everything I saw. I can't imagine what it could be, but for the sake of our family, I hope for it more than anything.

"I better get," I whisper from the doorway.

Evelyn doesn't turn around as she continues to stare at Madison. "I'll see you tonight," she whispers back.

I turn and leave, locking the condo door behind me. Madison is the only thing I think about on my drive to work.

21

After I leave, I resist the urge to call Evelyn on my drive. It's not something I would typically do, and I need to ensure I don't arouse any suspicion. I'm exhausted. A night of lying awake, puzzling out Evelyn's connection to Patty Dane, took its toll.

When I get to work, I head straight to my office, close the door and the blinds, and take a seat at my desk. I have a lot of time to think about what to do with the information I uncovered last night.

One option is to confront Evelyn with the evidence and allow her to explain. If Evelyn knew anything about Alison's murder, she also knew Lizzy was innocent, but Evelyn was willing to let her rot in prison for the crime.

The option I decide on comes with its own risks, though. I flip through my phone and find the detective's name who handled Alison's case. The last time I spoke to the detective, he alerted me of the overlooked DNA evidence and told me Lizzy would get a retrial as a result. The detective made no efforts to hide his opinion. The rest of the evidence against Lizzy was overwhelming, and he felt the right person was behind bars. Now though, I see some truth to Liz's version of the facts. Patty was Evelyn's patient. There is no way that connection is a coincidence.

I'm surprised when the detective picks up. Every other time I've reached out to him, I've left a voicemail.

"Hi, yes, I am so sorry to bother you, Detective. This is Nathan Foster," I say. "I don't know if you remember—"

"I know who you are, Mr. Foster. It's not often I have a case where a murderer goes free. How is your wife?" I assume he means Lizzy.

"Ex-wife," I correct him. "I'm remarried, though."

"I see." He sounds suspicious, but maybe I'm paranoid.

"That's why I am calling," I continue, hoping I am not making the biggest mistake of my life. "My new wife has been a nervous wreck since Liz's release."

"That's understandable, considering how things ended for your mistress." His words are cold.

"Yes, well, I was hoping maybe you could help me put her mind at ease." It is actually my mind I hope the detective soothes.

"I'm not sure what you mean," the detective replies.

"I was hoping you maybe had some new information about the DNA that was found at the crime scene." I don't know Evelyn's involvement with Alison or if she only found out about Patty and what she did after the fact, and she sought me out from someplace of guilt. I can't reveal my suspicions to the detective until I know more.

"And how exactly would that make your new wife feel better?" he inquires.

"Umm . . ." I regret the phone call instantly. "If there's another suspect, that would mean my wife won't have to worry so much about Liz being out."

The detective is quiet for a moment. "It's probably good for your wife to have a little healthy caution."

I sigh. I didn't believe Liz when she said she didn't kill Alison, even though I should have. I should have known she wasn't capable of actually killing someone. I don't see how Patty Dane came to know who Alison was, but Evelyn must know something she's not telling me. I owe it to Liz to figure this out for not being the husband she needed me to be.

"Yes, of course, but is there any reason my wife should worry about this Patty person?" I press. "If she was the one who killed Alison, I want to be certain she doesn't pose a threat to my new family."

"Look, sir," the detective huffs, and I notice he sounds annoyed. "DNA evidence is not as black and white as they make it appear on television. The opportunity for cross-contamination is high. It's not just at the lab. DNA can be transferred at the manufacturer, the store clerk; hell, just some shopper who picks up the knife to take a closer look could leave DNA."

"I thought they found blood on the weapon. Doesn't that seem like it's not just cross-contamination?" I know it wasn't some mistake in a lab because my new wife was Patty Dane's doctor, but I can't tell that to the detective without blowing up our lives. The police might even suspect I had something to do with Alison's death and think Evelyn and I hired Patty to frame my wife. I thought through all the scenarios, and very few ended well when it came to the detective and revealing too much. I will not risk Madison growing up without her parents.

"Mr. Foster, is there some reason you're so desperate to have it not be your first wife who killed your mistress?"

"Excuse me?"

"I'm just wondering if your new wife should be keeping a closer eye on you too." I am outraged at the detective's insinuations.

"Fuck you," I growl.

"What's wrong? Did I strike a nerve?"

"I want to make sure some crazy person is not out there posing a threat to my wife," I snap. "I saw in the news this Patty escaped from a mental treatment facility."

"Escape feels like a bit of an extreme term," the detective says. "There was a fire at the hospital she was a resident at, and in the chaos, she wandered off. My guess is her body will eventually turn up."

"Wait, you think she's dead?" I'm surprised by the statement.

"Doesn't that seem like a much more logical explanation as to what happened to Ms. Dane? The idea that she traveled from Georgia to Boston, Massachusetts, to murder the woman you were sleeping with, the one your wife just so happened to be stalking, feels a bit far-fetched. Don't you agree?" The detective had made up his mind about the guilty person regarding Alison's murder.

"Can you please do me a favor? If you hear any news in regard to Patty Dane, could you please reach out?"

"I can't do anything that would interfere with the

investigation. But if I have any reason to suspect you or your family might be in any danger, I won't be doing my job if I don't reach out," the detective rattles off matter-of-factly.

"Thanks, I guess," I mutter unenthusiastically.

"Mr. Foster, you don't seem to want to listen to me about this, but I will tell you all the same. If you care about your new wife, I would do whatever it takes to keep your ex-wife away from her."

"Thank you, Detective." I hang up the phone, frustrated I am no closer to figuring out how to uncover my wife's secrets.

22

Nathan: How's it going?

Evelyn: Good, Madison is in a great mood today.

Nathan: It must have been all that excellent quality time with her dad.

Evelyn: Maybe.

Evelyn: Are you leaving early today?

Nathan: I can't. I told you, I have meetings all day.

Evelyn: Okay.

Nathan: I'll be home as early as I can, I promise.

I wait for Evelyn to say something. Multiple dots appear on the screen and disappear, then nothing. She was going to say something and then thought better of it. Evelyn is growing impatient. I need to figure out what she's hiding before she forces my hand on this move to Michigan.

It's funny. I thought my life was complicated because I juggled a relationship with Lizzy and Alison at the same time. After the murder, I realized how complicated life could be. Now it feels so much worse with Madison caught in the middle of all of this. I can't see a way out. What if Evelyn found out about what her patient did to Alison after the fact? Perhaps, it was guilt that drew her to me. Was it innocent in the beginning? A desire to help me because she knew how a previous patient of hers had destroyed our lives. Would I take Madison's mother away because of it?

I bite my lip, conflict uncoiling in my stomach as I consider what I should do next. If the scenario was true and that was the explanation behind it, that would mean Evelyn was okay with letting Lizzy pay for the woman's crime and allowing Alison's real killer to remain free. Could I live with having a wife who was okay with punishing Lizzy? Did I want a mother like that around Madison?

I swallow hard. I need help unraveling all the lies.

Emily. I remember she was traveling to Georgia to talk to Evelyn's parents. Perhaps something they told her will help me figure things out with Evelyn.

Flipping through my recent calls, I find Emily's number and press it. A moment later, I hear her voice.

"I didn't expect you to be calling me," she chuffs.

"Yeah, well, I wouldn't if I didn't think I had any other choice."

"So I take it you're suspicious of the new missus after all?" Emily sounds as if she is taunting me.

"I didn't say that," I snap defensively, even though she's right.

"You wouldn't be calling me otherwise."

"Did you find out anything or not?"

"I did," she states, before silence fills the line. She's going to make me beg for it.

"And?" I draw out the word.

"Fine," she huffs. "First of all, her dad is definitely her biological father and not a stepdad."

"He said that?" I ask, more confused than ever why Evelyn would lie about that.

"Yup, I flat-out asked."

"What? How on earth did you explain that question?"

"I'm a reporter. I just acted like it was part of the question. I told them before we got started I just wanted to confirm they were both the biological parents of Evelyn Powell. They didn't suspect a thing," she explains.

"Did they say anything else?" I ask, the reality of just how much Evelyn lied to me sinking in.

"According to her parents, everything was good leading up to the move to Boston. They had a farewell dinner planned that she never showed up for. They even thought she went missing for a little while. That is until they reached out to the hospital in Boston, hoping someone had heard from her. That's when they found out she had, in fact, moved there without so much as a goodbye. She got a new phone number and wouldn't reply to any of their letters."

"Do they think it had anything to do with the fire at the hospital she was working at?"

"How do you know about the fire, Nathan?"

I gasp as my entire body stiffens. "I saw something about it."

"You know something, don't you?" she presses.

"I don't know what I know," I confess.

"I know you're hiding something."

"Will you please just tell me what else you found out?" I plead.

She huffs in frustration before she continues, "Her parents told me the fire happened the day after her last day. They think maybe Evelyn blames herself."

"For the fire?" I clarify.

"Uh-huh, they said she was extremely close to her patients, and they believe that one of her patients may have started the fire and then ran away. They believe that Evelyn might feel responsible for accepting the job in Boston."

"What does her going to Boston have to do with the fire?"

"Well, they can't be certain because Evelyn won't talk to them about it, but they think her leaving was a trigger for her patient."

"So what, Patty loses her shit that Evelyn will no longer be her doctor, lights the hospital on fire, and then follows her here?" I ask, thinking out loud. That would make sense of how Patty ended up in Boston, but not why she targeted Alison.

"Wait, what?" Emily asks, and I realize I revealed information she has not yet uncovered. Her parents obviously did not mentioned the patient's name that followed Evelyn to Boston. "Nathan, what do you know about Patty?"

I sigh, hoping I don't regret what I'm about to share. "I just found out."

"Damn it! I knew you knew something, you son of a bitch."

"I wasn't trying to hide it. I just found this out myself. Patty Dane was Evelyn's patient when she lived in Georgia. She was the one who disappeared after the fire," I reply.

"What? Oh, my God. Liz was right. Your psycho wife did have something to do with Alison's death."

"We don't know that," I insist, though it is starting to look like that is the case.

"Are you fucking kidding me? Have you told the detective?"

"I called him before you."

"What did he say?" she demands.

"He didn't seem like he wanted to listen to what I had to say, so we never got that far," I explain.

"Yeah." Emily laughs. "That guy can't get over the fact that he locked up an innocent woman. He would rather see Liz go back to prison than find the actual killer. What are you going to do?"

"What do you mean?"

"Oh, come on! Your wife was the doctor of the woman whose DNA was found on the murder weapon that killed your mistress," Emily snaps.

"Okay and . . .?"

"She had something to do with Alison's death!"

"Yeah, maybe," I admit.

Emily laughs. "Oh, come on, Nathan, you clearly did not meet this woman by happenstance. Are you going to sit there and tell me there's a reasonable explanation for all of this?"

"Let's say I think there's something to this—"

"Because there is, and she's a fucking murderer," Emily interjects.

I ignore her and continue. "If Evelyn does know something, what's your theory? Did she know about it before the murder? Did she only learn about it after, and that's why she tracked me down? Are you saying you think she's working with Patty?"

"Oh my God, this makes so much sense now." Emily gasps.

"What does?"

"I have to go," she says.

"Wait, I need to know, what makes sense?" I ask.

"I have to call Liz," Emily exclaims. "I hope you can now see that Evelyn is dangerous."

"I need to—" Emily hangs up before I can finish my statement. What did she figure out? What did she need to tell Liz so urgently? I try redialing Emily, but it goes to voicemail.

"Damn it," I say, slamming my fist down on the desk just as my door opens. Brad's assistant steps into my office after a brief knock. "Yes, what is it?" I ask impatiently.

"I'm sorry to disturb you, but your wife and daughter are here," she says.

I shake my head. "I'm sorry, you must be wrong," I reply. There is no way Evelyn is here. I was texting with her a few minutes ago. She's home with Madison.

The woman looks over her shoulder apprehensively and then back at me. From behind her, I catch sight of Evelyn holding the baby carrier. I jump up from my seat, my heart pounding as I race over to her.

"Evelyn," I gasp as Brad's assistant excuses herself

awkwardly. I take the carrier away from her. "I thought you were home."

"We wanted to surprise you," she chimes, studying my face. I check to see if I'm sweating as I guide her inside my office. "I texted you from the parking lot."

"Oh, well, you surprised me all right."

"I have to admit there's an ulterior motive for my visit," she confesses.

This is it. I'm found out. Evelyn knows I found the key to the storage locker. She's aware that I know her secrets.

"Oh?" I ask, gripping Madison's carrier a little tighter.

Evelyn sits down in the chair across from my desk and lifts her purse onto her lap. She reaches inside, and I instinctively put the carrier down onto the floor next to me to keep my daughter safe. Evelyn looks at me with a puzzled gaze as she pulls out a Tupperware dish.

"I know you said you're busy today, but I was hoping we could have lunch together," she says.

"Oh, of course, I would love that," I answer. I look down at Madison. "Do you mind being down there, sweetie, so that I can see Mommy better?" I ask in a high-pitched voice, trying to disarm any suspicions from Evelyn.

I look back at Evelyn. "I do have a one o'clock meeting, so I need to keep it short if that's okay?" The truth is I have no meetings. I need time to figure out what I'm going to do about Evelyn.

She nods. "Maybe we could talk about the move some more?"

"Sure," I say. "What about the move?"

"Well, I know you said you didn't like the idea of

living in a B&B, so I was wondering what you thought about buying one, but we would live in a separate house nearby. I could get up and head to the inn every day with Madison before you head to the office."

"I don't like the idea of exposing Madison to countless strangers," I argue, shaking my head. "I don't think it's a good idea."

"Why do you have to be like this?"

"Like what? I want to keep our daughter safe, that's all."

"That's exactly why I want to move in the first place. I don't feel safe raising her here when I know your crazy ex-wife is running around the city," Evelyn says, quickly growing agitated.

I press my lips together, determined not to reveal what I discovered before I figure out everything I need to. Lizzy made some mistakes, but she is no murderer. That much I'm sure of now. Evelyn seems determined to get me to see her in that light, though.

"They released her because a jury says she didn't do it," I remind her. Though, from her expression, I wish I hadn't.

"And now what, you suddenly believe her? Did you forget she threatened me when I saw her in prison? I guess that doesn't matter to you," Evelyn bellows, and I'm almost certain she's lying now about Liz threatening her. She lied to me about so much. It would make sense she lied about that as well. I wish I hadn't destroyed the copy of the letters between Evelyn and Lizzy Savannah brought me. Perhaps the insight could help me figure out exactly what my wife is lying about and what her motivation might be.

"No, of course not. Honestly, I don't know what Liz thought when that happened. Maybe she was just overwhelmed that day when you saw her because she had just signed the divorce papers. I'm certain she didn't mean it."

"Certain? Certain enough to gamble with the lives of your wife and child?"

"I think you're being a little dramatic, don't you?"

"Nathan . . ." Evelyn's mouth drops open.

"What?"

"Are you still in love with your ex-wife?" she asks.

"What?" Surprise envelops me, and I gasp.

She shakes her head. "I was worried about this," she says.

"What are you talking about?"

"I knew when she weaseled her way out of prison, she was going to convince you somehow that she was the victim in all of this."

"I never said I thought Liz was the victim," I argue.

"But you suddenly think maybe she didn't murder Alison."

"I don't know who killed Alison," I exclaim, fighting the urge to have it all out right here. I want to demand she tell me the role she played in everything. Was she aware of what Patty was going to do before she killed Alison, or did she only find out after? I look down at Madison. I can't, though, not yet. "Where is all this coming from?" I ask.

Evelyn starts to cry quietly. "I'm so stupid."

I move around the desk to stand next to Evelyn, leaving Madison behind the safety of my desk. "What are you talking about?"

"That's why you don't want to give your notice. You're trying to figure out how to leave me. You want to go back to Liz."

I kneel. "I'm not going back to Liz," I state firmly. "I simply don't want our kid raised around strangers at some B&B. I don't know how this turned into me wanting to leave you." Maybe she senses my doubt about her. Does she know that I discovered the storage locker?

"Do you mean it?" she asks as she wipes her tears away, looking into my eyes.

I smile at her. Hold it together.

"Of course I do. How about this? I'll give my notice by Friday," I offer, knowing I have until then to figure this out.

"Really?"

I nod. "I still don't like the idea of Madison being raised in a B&B, but how about if I agree not to take it completely off the table?" My offer doesn't matter. At this point, I need to buy time with Evelyn until I figure out exactly what her role was in Alison's death; I need to figure this out before I go to the police to ensure Maddie is protected.

"If you saw the place in person, you would change your mind," she adds before leaning forward and opening the Tupperware she brought.

"Maybe you're right," I answer before I proceed to have lunch with a woman who might have had something to do with the murder of Alison.

23

I have no one o'clock meeting with clients. What I do have is a timer on when Evelyn will figure out I'm looking into her past. I watch as she carries Madison out the door of my office, feeling helpless to solve the predicament I find myself in.

I consider calling the detective back. I hadn't met Evelyn when Alison was murdered. If Evelyn's patient was the one who killed her, that meant Evelyn was linked to the case, even if it was after the fact.

Closing my eyes, I think back to the final weeks of Alison's life. I have replayed those moments so many times, but it was in regard to Lizzy when I did. Did I miss something about Evelyn in my memories?

I turn to the computer and type Patty Dane into the search engine. I scan the articles for an image of her, but all I find is a blurry awkward childhood photo. Nothing that will help me remember if I ever saw her before Alison's death.

"Damn it," I mutter under my breath.

I lean back in my chair, trying to think of my next step. My mind drifts to Alison, then the crime scene photos. The image of the dark red pooling on the sheets around her makes me sick. I might hurl, so I bend over in the chair and place my head between my knees, focusing on my breathing.

I am relieved when my thoughts are interrupted by my phone buzzing. I look at the face, and it's a text message.

Emily: Liz is at her mom's.

I know it is an invitation to call Lizzy. To discuss with her the mystery that surrounds Evelyn and what happened to Alison. I haven't spoken directly to Lizzy, though, since I saw her in prison and warned her to stay away from Evelyn. I saw her in the courtyard of our home weeks prior, but she didn't wait around to speak to me. Here we are, though. We both want the truth, and we are each other's best hope to find it. I have a restraining order on her, though. If there is going to be a call, it has to come from me.

I flip through my contacts and stare at the number to Liz's mom as I try to work up the courage to dial it. Once I reach out to Liz, there is no going back. It's almost certain Evelyn will see it as a betrayal, especially after she expressed her concerns that I'm still in love with Lizzy. I need answers, though. There's too much now for me to ignore.

I press the name and listen as it repeatedly rings. "Nathan?" I hear my ex-mother-in-law's voice on the other end.

"Hey, sorry to bother you," I say. "Is there any chance

Liz is there?" I ask even though I already know the answer.

"Um, well, yes, she is." She sounds confused.

"I need to talk to her, please."

"In regard to what?" The confusion melts into a protective tone. It's funny to think how Lizzy needed to be protected from this woman most of her life, and here she is, acting like she's the one looking out for her daughter.

"It's important," I assure her.

"You're the one who got a restraining order against her," she continues. "I suppose if you have something important to discuss with her, you should have thought about that before you went and did that."

"Mom." I hear Liz's voice in the background, and it causes a flutter in my stomach. "Is that him?"

"I'll take care of it, sweetie. Don't worry," her mother says, though her voice is muffled. I am about to plead my case when I hear Liz again.

"Oh my God, Mom, give me the phone," she moans. After some rustling noises on the other end, I finally hear Lizzy say, "Hello?"

"Hey." I want to say so many things at this moment. I want to tell her I'm sorry I didn't believe her when she said she didn't kill Alison. I want to tell her I was the shit-tiest husband in the world, and for that, I'm sorry. She could never know how sorry I was. I don't say any of that, though. All I have is, hey.

"You know, don't you?" she replies. Her words hang between us like a noose. She knows if I'm calling her, it's for a good reason.

"I don't know what I know," I reply, surprised the sound of her voice relaxes me.

"She'll kill you if she thinks you know," Lizzy warns me.

"It's not that simple. We have a baby together."

She sighs. "I know, but it doesn't change the fact that your wife killed Alison. If she thinks her secret isn't safe, she'll do whatever she has to in order to protect it."

"That doesn't make any sense," I argue. "Evelyn's DNA wasn't found on the murder weapon."

"Even if she didn't actually kill her, she put the murderer up to it. How did you know Patty was her patient anyway?" Liz asks.

"I found newspaper clippings about a fire that had happened where Evelyn worked before Mass General. One of them said there was a missing patient. As soon as I saw Patty's name, I recognized it. The article said Evelyn was her doctor." I don't hesitate to share the information about my new wife. Before Maddie was born, I hated Liz. I was convinced she murdered Alison and our unborn child. I can't believe I could be so wrong.

"So what, you just found this article lying around the house?" she asks.

I hesitate. "Not exactly."

"What aren't you saying?" she presses.

"I don't know. It feels wrong to tell you all of this," I admit. "So much has happened in the past couple years."

"Yeah, like me going to prison for something I didn't do," she snaps.

"I know," I reply. "I'm sorry all of this happened to you." I want to tell her not only am I going to figure out what Evelyn had to do with this because I want to protect my daughter but also because Liz deserves to have her name cleared. I can't say any of that, though, because when it comes down to it, I'm not sure what I will do until I know exactly what Evelyn's involvement was.

"It's a little late for apologies," she states firmly. "I wouldn't be talking to you if you didn't have unfettered access to Evelyn." I'm not shocked by her words. I would hate me too.

I sigh. "I don't know what you want from me. I'm trying to figure out if Evelyn was involved, but I still don't know what she knew or when she knew it."

Lizzy laughs. "It's funny. When it was me, you were more than happy to think I was a murderer even though I swore to you I didn't do it."

"That's not fair. You weren't completely innocent."

"I'm not doing this with you. I thought you, of all people, would want to make sure the woman who was around your daughter wasn't a psychopath, but clearly, I overestimated the man you are once again." Her words cut me as if they were a blade.

"I'm being careful because of my daughter," I snap. "I was wrong about you, and you ended up paying a steep price. What if I'm wrong about Evelyn? My daughter would pay the price."

"She's a killer. She admitted it to me. What else do you want?"

"I want proof!" I exclaim. "Before I screw everyone's lives again, I have to be certain. I can't be wrong again."

"Why would she have said that to me?"

"I don't know," I admit. "Maybe she was angry, or

maybe she wanted to hurt you. Or maybe she felt like she was responsible because it was her patient who murdered Alison."

"If Patty did kill Alison, she put her up to it."

"We don't know that. We're talking about the mother of my child." My voice cracks as I start to plead with Liz. "For her sake, I need there to be zero doubt."

"I have zero doubt," Lizzy says with conviction.

"Well, I don't, and until I do, I won't let you hurt my family."

"Are you threatening me?" When I hear her question, it's like the wind is knocked out of me. Is that what this has come to? Is that what I am doing?

"No," I reply. "I'm asking you to help me prove who the killer is and what exactly Maddie's mother had to do with it."

"You want me to try to exonerate your wife?"

"No, I want you to help me find the truth, whatever it is. I didn't fight for the truth when it was you, and it's one of the biggest regrets of my life."

"What if the truth isn't what you want it to be?"

I think about her question. Am I willing to turn in the mother of my child if I find out she played a role in the murder of Alison? "Whatever we uncover, I won't stand in the way."

"You promise?" I'm surprised that my promise would mean anything to her now.

"I promise," I confirm.

She pauses for a moment, and the silence on the other end of the line is deafening. I don't know where else to turn. The idea that I'm asking my ex-wife for help to prove if my new wife has anything to do with the murder of my mistress is so messed up I can't even begin to process it. She's the only other person in the world, though, who wants to get to the truth as much as I do, even if it's for different reasons.

"What do you need my help with?" she asks at last.

"I found some articles in a storage locker that Evelyn hid from me," I start.

"What, how?"

"It's a long story, but when Evelyn was out of town, I snuck over there to take a look. But then she called me while I was there, and I was afraid she'd figure out where I was, so I left," I explain.

"You have to go back," Liz insists.

"That's just it. Evelyn's back in town, and I'm worried if I go back over there, she might figure out that I found the place."

"Then I'll go," Liz doesn't hesitate to offer.

"I can't believe I'm even talking to you about this," I admit out loud. "This doesn't feel real."

"Well, it is real," Liz interjects. "Just remember who you're doing this for." I know she's referring to Madison, but if I am completely honest, I'm also doing this for her. The best way I can think to say I am sorry for what I put her through is to help her clear her name once and for all.

"I know."

"All you have to do is let us in, then you can leave."

"Us?"

"I'll bring Savannah with me. The two of us can get through everything quicker. When we find something, I'll let you know, and then we can turn it over to the detective."

"If you find something," I attempt to correct her.

"Right, of course, if we find something."

I tried the detective. I can't see any other options. I need to know what else Evelyn is hiding. "I let you guys in, then I'm gone, okay?"

"I'll text you my new number from my mom's phone. Send me the location, and Savannah and I will meet you there in one hour," Lizzy instructs. Evelyn will never forgive me if I'm wrong, but I'm more afraid of what it will mean if I'm right.

I hang up. The number comes through, and I text the location of the storage locker back.

24

I glance at my phone as I sit behind the steering wheel, apprehension growing in my stomach. I imagine Evelyn sitting in the parking lot, watching, waiting for me to leave. She was different when she stopped at the office today. I have never sensed paranoia in her before. Everything felt off, and in my gut, I can't shake the feeling that her irrational accusations are because she senses my mistrust in her.

Dialing her number, I wait for her voice to come across the car speaker. "Miss me already?" she asks.

"Absolutely, I always miss my girls when I'm not with them." I need her to think everything is normal.

"Well, after the move, you can be with us all the time," she says.

I don't know what to say in response to that. "What are you two up to?"

Guilt gnaws at me because I don't miss her. She's my wife, and I should miss her. I don't want to admit to myself that I made a mistake. I've made more mistakes than I can count, but it's clear marrying Evelyn was one of my larger ones. Even if she isn't a murderer, it's become clear to me that you can't make yourself love someone. No matter how much I want to give Maddie the family I didn't have, it feels more and more like it's not something I will be capable of.

"It's a surprise." I hate surprises, especially ones planned by a woman I don't trust.

"Oh, come on, you can tell me," I say playfully in an attempt to disarm her.

"I promise it's good."

I need to know. Is her surprise that she can see me right now? I need to head to the storage locker, but I also need to know it's safe to do so. "I'm having a rough day at work. I bet knowing your surprise would cheer me up."

"I just saw you a couple hours ago. What's happened since then?"

"A rough call with a potential client. It looks like they're going another way." I roll into the lie effortlessly, making me think of what a hypocrite I am for being upset that Evelyn lies to me. I remind myself it's not the same. Her lies could hurt our daughter.

"Aw, babe, I'm so sorry. Look at the bright side. It will make it easier to give your notice, right?"

"True." I suppose it's good she still thinks I'm focused on this move. It might mean she doesn't suspect I'm looking into her after all. "So, what's this surprise?"

"Are you sure you don't want to wait?"

"Positive," I say with enthusiasm.

"Madison and I are in line at the butcher's down the

street from home. We're going to get something special to make you for dinner."

They aren't home, but she's also not sitting in the parking lot watching me.

"I don't deserve you."

"Don't be silly," she scoffs. "People deserve what they decide they deserve in life."

The statement is chilling to me. I would have thought nothing of it before my doubts, but now, it feels like she is saying so much more. I swallow and force myself to speak.

"Well, I'm glad I decided I deserved you, and you decided you deserved me." It feels wrong and forced as I say it.

"Will you be home on time?" she asks.

"How about I head home early and help you cook?" Evelyn isn't one to cook. Every night Lizzy would have a masterpiece waiting on the table for me when I got home. Evelyn is a pro at ordering takeout. It doesn't bother me, but it is hard to imagine her cooking an entire meal from scratch and it not ending up a total disaster.

"Really? I would love that." She sounds excited.

When I hang up the phone, I don't move. At my lowest, when I thought Lizzy had murdered my mistress, and it felt like I would never be able to face the world again, Evelyn helped put me back together. Was it all a lie?

It didn't feel possible. Evelyn had secrets; that much could not be denied, but to be involved in Alison's murder? The conflict of what I am about to do swirls in my head. Despite never planning to have a relationship with Evelyn, she did help me grieve. She made sense. She was stable in a way I hadn't experienced in my life. When I found out she was pregnant, I convinced myself marriage based on passion didn't work. Lizzy and I were evidence of that. Here I am, though, getting ready to blow up my marriage with Evelyn. Perhaps I'm the part of the equation that doesn't work.

"What are you doing?" I ask myself out loud as I grip the steering wheel.

My phone buzzes in the seat next to me. I pick it up and look at the screen.

Lizzy: We're on our way.

I instantly put the car in reverse and head in the direction of Beaumont Avenue. I try to clear my mind of the doubts of what I am about to do. My marriage with Evelyn might be over no matter what, so the least I can do is figure out what she's hiding and use the information to protect the people I care about.

25

W hen I pull and park in front of the storage facility, my hands tremble. I'm nervous, but I don't know if it's because I'm scared I might be married to a killer or because I'm about to see Liz again.

I look around, half expecting to see Evelyn standing here, waiting for me, but I'm alone. I think for a moment I can turn around and head straight home, help my wife cook dinner, spend time playing with my daughter, and put all of this behind me. Am I okay knowing I'll probably never actually love my wife? I'd told myself I was, but now I'm not so sure. Can I live with never knowing the truth? Can I accept that the mother of my child might be associated in some way with the death of a lover I once had? What kind of person am I if I can accept that?

My thoughts are interrupted by a knock on the driver's side window. I jump, my head jerking to see the girl I previously met at my office standing there, peering down at me. I roll down my window.

"Savannah, right?" I ask.

She nods but doesn't say anything. She glances around, taking in her surroundings. She bites her lip apprehensively, and I can tell she's nervous too.

I look behind her. She seems to be alone. "Where's Liz?"

"Are you alone?" she asks, taking a step back from my door. I climb out of the car.

"Do I look alone?" I reply, looking around at the empty parking lot.

She narrows her eyes at me. "Just answer the question."

"Yes, I'm alone," I answer. She takes a couple steps back, and I wonder if she's scared of me. I don't know what Lizzy has told her, but considering I didn't exactly stand by her after the trial, I'm confident it isn't good.

"You know, I'm the one who has the most to lose in this situation. If Evelyn finds out, I'm here . . ."

"Save it," she grunts as she turns and looks toward the multiple dumpsters positioned on the side of the property and waves her arms.

Squinting my eyes, I watch as a figure steps out from behind the dumpsters. It's Lizzy. My stomach flutters as she walks toward me. Her hair is shorter than I remember, but she's as stunning as ever with the blond strands framing her face. She seems thinner, the stress of prison and the last couple of years have likely taken their toll on her. I liked her curvy frame, but the more slender version of her is still just as striking.

My chest tightens as she walks toward me. My face is hot, and I feel my eyes grow wet. What is happening to me? Savannah whispers something to Liz, and I watch their interaction. Liz wraps a protective and reassuring arm around the young girl; they're close. Lizzy has an entirely new life now. She has friends I don't know. Close friends who would risk themselves to help her. I can't think of anyone in my life who would help me at their own peril. Since marrying Evelyn, I'm isolated. I have my golf games with Travis and work. The one outing I had with friends was the bachelor party I went to when I missed the birth of my child. None of those people I surround myself with, though, would show up for me if I needed them. Not like the way people show up for Lizzy.

I'm embarrassed and full of regret that I couldn't see Lizzy was innocent when others obviously could. She created a fierce loyalty in this new friend, even after she didn't receive it from her husband.

With all the changes in her appearance, something about her still feels like my Lizzy. I watch her talking to Savanah and remind myself she's not my Lizzy anymore. She will never be my Lizzy again. I focus my thoughts on Madison, reminding myself why I'm here.

"Nathan," Lizzy finally says with a nod in my direction, and I notice her jaw tense. She loathes me. It's written all over her face.

"Hey, Liz," I reply and start walking in the direction of the storage locker. The last thing I want is to chance someone I know driving by and seeing me standing outside, talking to my ex-wife. "It's this way."

The two women follow me through the door, and we make our way around the labyrinth of halls until we reach the familiar unit. Liz is standing right behind me as

I retrieve the key from my pocket. I hesitate, staring at the lock.

"What's wrong?" Savannah asks.

I swallow hard and turn to look at the woman who was my wife, the woman I betrayed multiple times by having an affair and then not believing her when she said she didn't kill Alison.

"I'm sorry." The words escape in a tiny squeak. I clear my throat and repeat them.

Lizzy says nothing. She's staring at the key in my hand.

"Did you hear what I said?" I ask, shaking my head. "I'm so sorry I didn't believe you."

She doesn't look at my face when she answers, her eyes still locked on the key in my hand. "There's a lot we should both be sorry for, but right now, none of that matters."

I want her to hear me, to understand how terrible I feel about everything she went through. "I just wanted you to know I realize I should have believed you."

Her shoulders tense. "Yes, you should have. Now can you please open it?"

I nod. She has no desire to talk about what happened. Honestly, I'm not sure I'm ready to talk about it either. I was compelled to say I'm sorry in person. It seems like something she deserves to hear face-to-face.

I slide the key into the lock before lifting the gate.

My stomach sinks. I step back and double-check the locker number, but the key worked, so I already know I'm right. Lizzy steps inside, switching the light on.

"I don't understand," she says.

"I told you he was wasting your time," Savannah snaps.

"I was just here. It doesn't make sense," I say as I look around the empty unit. There isn't even a scrap of paper left on the floor. "This was full a couple days ago."

"This means she knows," Liz says, looking at Savannah.

I shake my head. "I had lunch with her today, and I just got off the phone with her. She acted like everything was completely normal." I turn around in circles, trying to process what I'm seeing. I recount everything I saw. The articles referencing Patty as a patient of Evelyn, the old photos, it had all been here.

Lizzy laughs. "You obviously don't know who you're dealing with."

"What am I going to do?" I gasp as the reality of the situation sinks in. If the storage locker is empty, Lizzy is right. Evelyn knows I found it.

"You need to protect your daughter, do you understand me? Evelyn is crazy," Lizzy warns as she narrows her gaze at me.

"No," I say, shaking my head. "This has to be some sort of a mistake." I say it more to convince myself, but I know it's not.

Liz ignores my panic and says, "I have a friend I can call who can help with this."

"A friend, what does that mean?" I ask.

"Someone I met in prison," Lizzy replies matter-of-factly.

"Are you sure?" Savannah whispers. "You can't take it back once you call her."

"Do you have a better idea?" Liz asks, staring at her friend.

"Wait, stop," I say, waving my hands. "I don't like the sound of this. We're talking about the mother of my child here."

"Yeah, well, she's a killer," Lizzy adds pointedly.

"We don't know that," I insist.

"Are you kidding me right now?" Lizzy laughs, gesturing toward the empty locker.

"She clearly has some sort of involvement. I'm not denying that," I argue. "I'm just saying maybe she cleaned this out because she was afraid I would uncover the connection she had to Patty. Maybe it's still not as bad as we think."

"Look, I get it, this is some scary-ass shit you're facing here, and I have tried to be patient with you, but I am not going to let this woman get away with taking my life from me."

I freeze, the memory of what Evelyn told me Lizzy said to her in prison filling my mind. "You know, Evelyn told me you threatened her the last time she saw you in prison. She said that you told her she wasn't going to get away with stealing her life from her."

Liz stiffens. "And she's not."

"Look, your wife is a psychopath," Savanah snarls, stepping between Liz and me. "It doesn't matter what Liz said to her because she's the one who killed your girlfriend."

"Who are you again?" I snap, not hiding my irritation.

"I'm someone who actually has Liz's back," she quips.

"Fuck, Liz, I'm not saying Evelyn is innocent. It's clear

she is somehow involved in what happened to Alison, but I don't like the sound of you calling someone to take care of the problem. I mean, holy shit, it sounds like you're putting a hit out on her or something."

"I mean, I should. That's what she deserves," Liz huffs.

"Are you kidding me? What happens if Maddie gets caught up in all of this and gets hurt?" I look at Liz as if I genuinely don't recognize her anymore.

She takes a deep breath. "Oh my God, Nathan, nobody is putting a hit out on your wife. I know you don't want to believe it, but Evelyn is the one who's a threat to your baby. I told you before. I'm not a killer. I know some people who can look into Evelyn, and maybe they can figure out if she's hiding something else."

"You won't hurt her?" I clarify.

Liz rolls her eyes. "No, nobody will hurt her."

I exhale a breath of relief, moving out of the locker and locking it back up after the women exit. "I can't believe this is happening."

"Well, it is. Go home, act like everything is normal, and I'll be in touch as soon as I hear something," Liz instructs me.

"Seriously? How am I supposed to do that?" I ask.

"I'm not exaggerating when I say your life is in danger," Lizzy adds before she and Savannah head toward a rear exit. "She knows you know about the locker. If she thinks you know too much, I don't know what she'll do. Don't call me. I'll call you after I know something."

I nod and watch them leave, waiting a few minutes before I head to my car so we are not exiting at the same time.

26

E velyn knows. As I drive to the condo from the storage facility, the fact takes hold in my brain. It's the only explanation for why she emptied the locker so quickly after my seeing it. She couldn't know what I saw, I tell myself. I was careful to return everything just as I found it. At least, I think I was.

I finally work up the courage to exit the safety of my car and head to our condo. Part of me expects Evelyn to be waiting for me at the door, ready to pounce. To my surprise, she's in the kitchen with a bottle of wine open on the counter. The ticking sound of Madison's swing sounds in the background. Evelyn glides around the kitchen rinsing vegetables and prepping her cook space. She's humming. Would a woman who thought her husband might suspect her of being involved in a murder be humming?

"You're in a good mood," I say, watching her as she places a bowl in the sink and starts to peel the potato in her hand.

She glances up at me briefly and smiles. "Am I?" She pauses to ponder the statement. "I guess I am."

I'm confused. Could she be this good at pretending, or did I completely misread everything? Is there nothing to the storage locker? Could it be that she had always planned to clear it out? We were planning to move after all. In addition to the boxes, there had also been old furniture in the unit. Did she donate everything in anticipation of the move?

"When you said you were getting home early, I didn't realize you meant this early," she states, not taking her eyes off the potato.

"Would you rather I go away and come back?" I ask in a teasing voice.

"No way. I love when you're home." She glances up and notices I'm hiding something behind my back. She suddenly stops peeling and watches me with a puzzled stare.

I reveal a bouquet I purchased on the way home. Unfortunately, my motivation isn't selfless nor romantic. I had the thought that if someone we knew saw me near the storage facility and mentioned it to Evelyn, it would confirm what I'd been up to. I picked up the bouquet at a nearby florist to cover my tracks.

"Travis told me this was the best florist in town, so I grabbed them on my way home," I lie.

She relaxes and smiles at me. "Aw, that's sweet, thank you." She doesn't take them from me. Instead, she returns to peeling.

I place them on the counter. "Let me change out of my work clothes, and I'll put them in some water."

She nods, only half acknowledging me. Once in the bedroom, I race to Evelyn's bedside table and replace the key I'd taken from the frame. On my way home, I debated if this was a prudent move. Evelyn obviously has access to the unit. She might have a spare key and have no idea the key I have was ever missing. There is also a chance she discovered it was missing and got a replacement, meaning by replacing the key, I might confirm any suspicion it was taken rather than misplaced or lost. In the end, I'm safer not possessing the key myself. I sigh a breath of relief and stare at the photo in the frame. It's of me holding Madison the week she was born. This is my family. Evelyn is my family. I turn, and my heart stops when I see Evelyn standing in the doorway. I give an audible yelp.

"You scared me," I say, forcing a smile.

She looks at me, saying nothing. How long was she there? What did she see? I can't tell from her expression what she's thinking. I hold my breath, waiting for her to say something, anything that will tell me I haven't just blown up my life.

"I didn't think to ask if you prefer the skins on or off for your mashed potatoes. I still have some I can leave the skin on if you like that better," she says at last.

"Both ways sound good to me." I smile and start to unbutton my shirt.

She turns and walks back to the kitchen, and for a second, I think I'm going to be ill. I grip the edge of the bed and steady my breathing. I finish changing and join Evelyn in the kitchen. Silently, I place the flowers in the vase and then start to play kitchen assistant.

Evelyn acts as if everything is fantastic. She shares stories of how great the butcher was and how he tossed in an extra lamb shank because he said Madison was too cute not to. I agree with the butcher. When Madison awakes, I tend to her as Evelyn continues talking. She tells me she's sure she wants to quit her job at the hospital and can't wait to leave the stress behind. She's ready to focus on her family and the move to Michigan. She doesn't bring up the bed and breakfast, though I keep expecting her to.

I have trouble focusing on her words when she talks. Instead, my mind is filled with questions. What does she know about Alison's death? Does she feel guilty about not stopping Patty? Is that the truth behind what is driving her decision to leave Boston? Does she know where Patty is?

I feed Madison and place her in a bouncy seat, flipping a Friends episode on low volume so I can go back and finish helping Evelyn in the kitchen. When I turn around, I see Evelyn placing candles on the dining table and lighting them.

"Everything always looks better by candlelight, don't you think?" she asks.

"I suppose," I reply, heading to the kitchen and helping her carry the plates to the table. I sit across from her. My mind is a mess with racing thoughts. I can't imagine her being so cool if she actually thought I might know of her connection to Patty. There are so many things I wish I could ask Evelyn. Is Patty still out there? Does she pose a threat to our family or Liz?

"It looks delicious," I say, noticing how dry the lamb is

as I cut into it. I top it with the sauce she has on the table. "Thank you for all your hard work."

She nods, slipping a bite into her mouth. Her eyes are fixed on me as she waits for me to take a bite. I pause, waiting for her to swallow her bite first. When she does, I feel safe enough to take a bite into my mouth. The delicious sauce helps mask the dryness of the lamb.

"Tastes as good as it looks," I add after I swallow the bite, a little surprised the sauce is so good. I feel like an actor playing a role, trying to convince the audience I'm the happy husband.

"Thank you," she says, glancing over her shoulder to ensure Madison is still engaged in her show before she continues eating.

I'm not the happy husband, though. The truth is, I feel sick sitting across from this woman. A realization set in on my drive to the condo that evening. The DNA evidence was missed at Lizzy's initial trial. That means Evelyn sought me out before Lizzy's new attorney discovered the oversight. The best-case scenario is that Evelyn tracked me down out of some sense of righting her guilt. How did she know Patty had killed Alison? Did Patty tell her what she did? It was the only explanation for seeking me out. If that was the case, she engaged in a relationship with me, and went to prison and spoke to Liz about our marriage, all while knowing the real killer was still out there. Even if Evelyn isn't the actual killer, she is a monster.

"What's going on in that head of yours?" Evelyn's voice cuts through my thoughts.

Oh, nothing. Just that I hate you.

"Huh?" I gasp. "Oh, nothing."

"You're being so quiet."

"I guess I'm just thinking about work," I lie.

"I know it's hard to tell your bosses you're leaving," she interjects.

I nod, relieved she seems to be so eager to accept the explanation of my distraction. "It won't take long before word gets to my father once I give my notice."

"He only has the control you allow him to have," she says.

I silently wonder if the same is true for Evelyn. Is the control she seems to have over my life only there because I allow her to have that power? I'm done giving people control over my life.

"I know what you said, and I respect it, but I got a call from the real estate agent about the B&B. She says the listing goes live at the end of this week. We could put an offer in on it before it's public," she says, and I'm surprised she waited so long to bring it up.

"Evelyn." I place my fork down onto my plate and look her in the eyes. "I don't think it's a good idea. There are so many crazy people in the world, and I don't like the idea of letting my daughter be around strangers day in and day out." She's probably the stranger I'm the most worried about right now.

Evelyn stands and walks over to me. She sits on my lap and wraps her arms around my neck, and I don't know how to react. I glance around, eyeing the knife I used to cut the lamb. I could grab it and protect myself if I needed to.

She kisses me, first softly, then deeply, before she pulls away.

"What was that for?" I ask, wondering if she can sense I'm nervous.

"I just love how much you love our family." She's taking this better than I imagined.

"I love Madison more than I ever thought was possible," I state, hoping she doesn't pick up on the fact she isn't included in the statement.

"I want you," she says, looking into my eyes.

I shake my head. "Want me to what?"

She laughs. "I want you to make love to me." When she says the statement, it takes everything in me not to have a physical reaction of disgust. I had so much time to think this all out, and there is no scenario where Evelyn is justified in any of her involvement in what happened with Alison.

"But Madison is right there," I point out, hoping she will let it drop.

"She's fine. She's in her bouncy seat. We'll hear her if she gets upset," she presses, standing and taking my hand, guiding me to our bedroom. "We'll even leave the door open to make sure we can hear her."

What do I say and not make it sound suspicious? How can I tell her the last thing I ever want to do is have sex with her again? There's nothing I can say. I'm stammering through excuses as she guides me to the bedroom, and despite my best efforts to push her away, we're eventually naked together on the bed. She attempts to give me an erection, but I can't get hard. She looks upset. I close my eyes and picture Lizzy's face, but even that is not enough.

"What's wrong?" she asks.

"I guess I had too much wine with dinner," I say. She accepts the answer, but I doubt she believes it. I am running out of time with Evelyn. If Lizzy can't figure something out soon, I may have no other choice but to confront her.

27

The following day, I awake by the sound of a door slamming. Evelyn is not in bed next to me. I glance at the clock and realize I'm already late for work. I hop up and start getting dressed, and when I turn around, Evelyn enters the bedroom.

"What was that noise?" I ask.

She doesn't say anything as I slide my slacks on and tuck my shirt into the waist. "I'm surprised it didn't scare Madison."

"Bridget took her on a walk," Evelyn answers in a quiet voice.

"I can't believe I forgot to turn the alarm on," I state, remembering the second bottle of wine we cracked the night before. "I wish you would have woken me up when you got up."

She's still quiet. I exit our closet and move to stand at the foot of our bed. Evelyn is sitting on her side of the bed, staring at the floor. I can see her reflection in the mirror over the dresser. She's been crying.

"What's wrong?" I ask.

"How long has it been going on?" Her voice cracks as she asks the question. She knows. She knows about me breaking into the storage locker. She knows Emily went to see her parents. She knows I discovered all her lies.

"I can explain," I start.

"Did you start sleeping with her as soon as she was released?" Her head snaps in my direction as she spits the words at me.

I shake my head in confusion. "Wait, what? What are you talking about?"

"You know, people told me there was no way you had changed and I shouldn't trust you. I told them that they were wrong; I knew the real you." The statement strikes me as funny, considering how little we know each other. Her glare at my reaction stops my laughter cold, and I stumble back a few steps.

"I have no idea what you're talking about."

"Don't lie to me. I saw your phone. You're having an affair with Liz," she snaps at me, her fists balled at her sides.

"No, I'm not!" I exclaim. I deleted any messages between Liz and myself after leaving the storage facility yesterday. If Evelyn saw something on my phone, it had to be recent. Did Liz already find something out?

"I can tell you've been distant, but I thought it was just the stress of work and the move."

"I am stressed about work and the move!" I repeat. "I'm also not having an affair and certainly not with my ex-wife."

"She texted you this morning wanting to know if you

were okay," she growls at me. I hope that's all the texts reveal.

"When we married, I gave you the passcode to my phone because I told you I never wanted you to think I wasn't fully committed to this marriage," I say, attempting to defuse the situation.

"Then why is she texting you? Have you seen her since she was released?"

I think about the question. What reasonable explanation can I have as to why she's texting me? I can't tell her Liz is helping me look into Evelyn's secrets. "No, of course not. She wanted to reach out to give me her number in case I needed to contact her about the investigation into Alison."

"What are you talking about?" Evelyn snaps. "Why would you need to talk to her about Alison's case?"

"Apparently, the detective was in contact with her about Alison's case. She thought I would want to know that the police are still actively investigating who is behind Alison's murder. That's it."

"Then why is she asking if you're okay?"

"Are you kidding me? You know as well as I do that Liz isn't stable. I have no idea why she's asking me that," I lie. I know Liz is asking because she's scared of what Evelyn might do, and I am too now.

"It's like I don't even know you," she says as she stands and turns to face me.

"To be fair, we do barely know each other." I see her face flush red, and I immediately regret the statement.

"You knew me well enough to marry me," she hisses.

I take a couple of steps back. "I wasn't exactly in a normal headspace when I agreed to marry you."

"Agreed?" she shouts. "Are you saying that I convinced you to marry me?"

"No, that's not what I meant." But that was precisely what I meant, and I'm tired of pretending.

"Then please, Nathan, enlighten me to exactly what you meant."

I rub a hand over my face before I take a deep breath and move close to Evelyn. I reach out and grip her arm, and she stiffens at my touch. "All I meant was when we got together, everything was crazy in my life, and maybe because of the place I was in, we probably moved faster than we should have."

"Do you regret marrying me then?"

"I didn't say that." But it was exactly what I meant.

"You were engaged to Liz after only three months and married to her after knowing her less than a year. I guess it wasn't a crazy time with her."

"Look how that turned out." My voice is elevated.

"Are you saying you want a divorce? Is that it?"

"What?" The question catches me off guard. "No, I never said anything like that."

"It sure feels that way."

"I mean, I have a lot of questions," I admit.

"Like what?"

I know I shouldn't ask, but I've come too far to stop now. "Like did you tell Liz that you killed Alison?"

"What? Are you serious?"

"I know it sounds crazy, but she says you told her that."

"When did she tell you that?"

"Yesterday."

"I thought you didn't see her." She glares at me as though she caught me red-handed.

"I haven't," I clarify. "She told me that when she called me about the detective and Alison's case."

"See, that's just it. You're having conversations with your ex-wife on the phone, and you don't think that's something you should mention to me?" Her nostrils flare. I have never seen her this angry. "I'm supposed to be your wife, Nathan."

"I was going to tell you, but I didn't want you to worry," I say, even though I never had any intention of sharing my conversation with Liz.

"She isn't supposed to call you, Nathan. That's what a restraining order is for," Evelyn fumes.

"I know, I'm sorry."

"I'm not going to let you pull Madison and me into this messed-up relationship you have with your ex-wife."

"I would never let anything happen to Madison, and you know that," I reply defensively.

"You're so blind. You're so obsessed with Liz you can't see what she's trying to do."

"What are you talking about?" I catch myself before I roll my eyes.

"What if she convinces this detective that I had something to do with Alison's death? Don't you see what that means?" She's yelling now.

"How could she do that?" I bait her.

"She's crazy. I wouldn't put it past her to plant evidence that I was involved. She'll do whatever it takes to get you back."

"I don't think that's what she's doing."

"You and I both know how bad Liz wanted to be a mother. She's delusional, Nathan. In her mind, if I am out of the way, it will open the way for the two of you to rekindle your relationship, and who do you think would become the mother to Madison?"

"That would never happen. You are Madison's mother."

I have to admit, Evelyn has a solid theory. Lizzy was destroyed when we lost Matthew. When she found out Alison was pregnant, she planned to murder her. Even if she changed her mind at the last minute, it didn't change the fact that it put her out of her mind.

Evelyn laughs slightly. "It's so insane to me that you're so worried about owning a B&B and the danger of strangers around our child, but you don't seem to see the evil you're inviting into our lives through Liz."

"I will never let anyone hurt Maddie. Do you hear me?"

"You may not be able to stop her," she warns.

"What do you mean?"

Evelyn hesitates.

"What is it?" I press. "You have to tell me."

"I thought she was just venting, but now I'm not so sure."

"Who, Liz?" I ask.

She nods. "The last time I went to see Liz in prison, she told me someone very powerful on the outside was going to help her get out."

I instantly think of my father when Evelyn says the words. Could he have that much power? Could he be capable of helping free Liz?

"Did she say who?"

Evelyn shakes her head. "No, just that they were capable of anything, and that if I didn't stop talking to you, I would regret it."

"That doesn't make sense. Nobody can be that powerful," I argue.

"Can't they?" Evelyn lifts her brows.

"I just can't see how that can be true."

"There you go defending her again."

"I'm not defending her."

"Do you want to hear how scary your precious Liz is? Do you remember our date at the restaurant a few weeks ago? I went to the restroom but then said I checked on the baby, and we left."

"Yeah, of course, I do." And I do remember. That was when I started having doubts about Evelyn and suspected that she was hiding something from me. She told me the sitter said Madison was fussy, but the sitter told me Madison had been great all night. Evelyn lied to me.

"Liz was there," Evelyn says.

"What? Where?"

"At the restaurant. I saw her over your shoulder, so I went to confront her." As she recounts the evening, it makes sense. Evelyn was visibly upset when she got back to the table. If she had a run-in with Liz that night, it would have made her react that way. "She told me if I didn't get out of her way, I would be the one who found herself in prison. I told her she was crazy, but she told me the same people who helped her get out would also help her put me away."

While we were at the storage facility, Liz said she had someone she needed to call. Someone who would help her expose Evelyn. Is that what she meant? Had I been an idiot? Is all of this part of Liz's plan?

I shake my head. "No, it can't be."

"Why? Because your precious Liz can't possibly be that diabolical?"

"How do you know Patty Dane?" I ask. There it is. The question is out, and there is no coming back from it.

"What?" She shakes her head. "I had a patient once by that name."

"And you didn't think to mention that when it came up at the trial that Patty's DNA was discovered at Alison's crime scene?" I'm pacing now.

Evelyn seems genuinely confused. "It can't be the same Patty. She's missing." She's shaking her head insistently now.

"And what about the storage locker?" I bite the words out at her, feeling relieved that Maddie is out on a walk with Bridget.

"What storage locker?"

"Oh, come on, Evelyn." I throw my hands up as I storm across the bedroom and toss the frame onto the bed. "The one I found the key for, hidden inside this frame."

She furrows her brows as she picks up the frame and retrieves the key. "Nathan, I have never seen this key before in my life."

"Stop lying," I shout. "It was rented in your name."

"I'm not lying." Evelyn starts to cry. "This has to be Liz. She must be the one behind all of this. I can't believe it.

I'm going to lose Madison." She covers her face with her hands. She's trembling.

"Are you trying to say Liz rented that unit, planted stuff to make it look like it was yours, all so I would think you were somehow involved?"

"I don't know, maybe." Evelyn whimpers.

"How did she get the key behind the picture frame?" I press.

"She figured out how to get out of prison. I doubt breaking into our condo would be too hard for her." Evelyn snorts, grabbing a tissue from the nightstand to wipe her nose.

I shake my head, trying to make sense of the story Evelyn clings to. The detective is convinced Liz is still guilty of the murder, but I don't know what to believe anymore. Could Liz really be working with someone powerful she met in prison or even my father?

"This is crazy," I state.

Evelyn stands and rushes to the closet, pulling out a suitcase.

"What are you doing?" I ask.

"I'm not going to sit around here and wait for your crazy ex-wife to have me put away for something I didn't do," she gasps. "I'm taking Maddie, and we're getting the hell away from here."

"You can't," I gasp desperately. The idea of losing Madison ties my stomach into knots. I reach out and grab her wrists.

She shakes her head at me, her cheeks stained with tears. "We can't stay here. It's not safe."

"Look in my eyes and tell me you had nothing to do

with Alison's death," I demand, not releasing my grip.

Her brows stitch themselves together, and I can see the hurt in her gaze as she looks at me. "I had nothing to do with that."

I swallow hard. I have a decision to make. I'm at a crossroads, and what I do now could be the difference between me being in my daughter's life or not.

"I'll give my notice today."

"What?" Evelyn is confused.

"If you say you didn't have anything to do with it, I believe you. It's my job to keep you safe. I'll quit my job, and we'll move," I add, my heart pounding in my chest.

"Do you mean it?" Evelyn cries as she rushes forward, burying her head into my chest. "I'm so sorry I ever doubted you."

28

I use my hip to push the front door open, carrying a large bundle of boxes inside the condo. I'm confident we did not need this many boxes when we moved into this place. I assume it's all the baby items we added after Madison arrived. It won't shock me if the baby items take up half the space on the truck.

"I come bearing gifts," I call, kicking the door closed behind me.

"Oh, I'm glad you're back," Evelyn says, rushing in to give me a hand with the boxes. "The real estate agent called. She said she needs you to sign the addendum on the Tudor."

That's what Evelyn calls the house I shared with Lizzy —the Tudor.

"She also says she may have an offer on one of the investment properties," Evelyn adds.

"Wow, she's earning her commission," I remark. The truth is this woman is one of the few realtors willing to take on listing the house Alison was killed in. I couldn't set foot in the place after what happened, but she took care of everything, including shipping all of Alison's belongings to her family.

"Great, I'll check my email and get them signed."

Evelyn tapes together one of the boxes and loads it full of items from the opened kitchen drawers. "I can't believe we're actually doing this," she says.

"I can't believe you wouldn't let me hire someone to pack all this." I smirk at her with a mischievous grin.

"Don't be silly. The condo isn't that big. We can pack it ourselves," she says. "So how is your first full day of no longer being gainfully employed?"

"Gee, when you put it that way, I kind of feel like a loser." I laugh.

"Stop it," she says as she tosses a towel in my direction.

I shrug. "I'm so busy I don't think it's hit me yet."

"That's understandable."

"How about you? Are you ready to wrap up your last cases?"

"You have no idea!" she exclaims. "Just cutting back is already amazing, but I will be so relieved when my replacement is ready to take over completely."

"You won't miss it?" I ask, taping together another box.

"I suppose." She shrugs. "I like the idea of helping people, but I'm not sure I truly have helped very many people."

"Don't say that. You helped me."

She smiles. "Thank you. Now take a box and start packing up our bedroom."

"Yes, ma'am," I chime and head in the direction of the master suite.

In the past two weeks, I became an expert at pretending everything is okay. Evelyn seems to believe me, and that's the way it needs to be for now. Shortly after my conversation with Evelyn, in which I revealed I knew about the storage locker, I purchased a burner phone. I've tried to reach Lizzy for the past few days, but there has been no response.

I don't buy the story that Evelyn thought it was just a coincidence that DNA found on the knife used to kill Alison just happened to belong to someone with the same name as a previous patient. What was even more absurd to me was the idea that someone staged the storage locker and planted a key in our home. For the sake of buying time for Liz's contacts to figure out precisely what else Evelyn is hiding, though, I have let Evelyn assume I gullibly swallowed every morsel of her tale. As far as Evelyn is concerned, we are packing up our lives to start a new adventure.

The truth is, I've started to panic a little. The last time I spoke to Liz was at the storage facility. Since then, it has been radio silence despite multiple efforts to reach out to her. If I don't hear from her soon, I will have to reach out to Emily. If not, I may find myself moving to Michigan to keep this charade going.

"Nathan," Evelyn calls from the kitchen. "The Michigan real estate agent wants to know what day we will be arriving to tour prospective homes."

The Michigan real estate agent. I am running out of time. If I don't figure out a way to expose Evelyn's involvement with Alison's murder soon, I'm unsure what I will do. There has to be clear evidence so there is no question when approaching the detective. If I want to have any shot at a life raising my daughter without Evelyn, I need to make sure she is locked away for the role she played in Alison's death. Sometimes, I feel heartless for the way I'm plotting behind her back, but then I remember all the things I already know she's lied about.

I worried my entire life about being like my father when I should have been worried I would turn out like my mother. She let him treat me the way he did. She allowed him to victimize me over and over. I can see that now that I am a parent. I will do whatever it takes to protect Madison, including putting her mother behind bars.

"It's a little crazy with all the packing and closings going on this week. How about one day next week?" I call back.

"Okay, I'll tell her," Evelyn chimes.

I turn my attention to filling the box in front of me. After it's full, I head back out to the kitchen for another box. "How are we already down to four boxes?" I ask. "I just brought ten up."

"Blame Madison. All of her toys are so large."

"Shame on you for blaming our precious little girl," I say.

"Babe, do you mind going down and grabbing ten more out of the basement?"

"No can do. That was the last of them."

"What? No, the guy at the moving company told me this would be enough." Evelyn is starting to panic.

"Never fear," I announce as I scoop up my keys from

the countertop. "I will run to the hardware store and pick up another dozen."

She looks around the room and frowns. "Better make it two dozen."

"Two dozen boxes, coming up," I announce, placing my hands on my hips and puffing out my chest.

"My hero!" she squeals, but just as she does, Madison starts to cry. "I can take care of her before I go," I offer.

"No, no," she says, waving her hands in my direction. "I'll feed her while you're gone, then we can keep packing together when you get back."

"Oh, lucky me." I grimace before laughing. I make sure the door locks behind me and head to my car. I look up directions to the closest hardware store on my phone. As I do, I jump when the phone rings. I assume it's probably Evelyn adding items onto my shopping list. I'm surprised when I see Liz's mom's name on caller ID. I hit the button on my steering wheel to connect the call over Bluetooth.

"Nathan?" I hear her voice.

"Yes, this is him," I answer.

I immediately hear sobbing on the other end of the line, and panic overwhelms me. "Michelle." I say her name, trying to calm her down. "What's wrong?"

I'm still met with hysteria.

"Has something happened?" I ask.

She sucks in a breath and chokes before she clears her throat and, through tears, tells me, "Liz was the victim of a hit-and-run."

"What? When? Is she okay?" The questions rapid-fire out of me.

"No, she's not okay," she yelps.

"Where is she?" I ask, my heart pounding wildly.

I hear Michelle gulp on the other end of the line before continuing. "She's been in a medically induced coma for the past two weeks." I understand now why I have not heard from Lizzy.

"No, that can't be right," I state, trying to convince myself that I must have misheard her.

"I'm so sorry. I wouldn't have called. I know you have a new family now, but I just thought you should know."

"I don't understand," I gasp, and I can feel myself start to shake as I grip the wheel tighter. "How did this happen?"

"She was walking in the parking garage at the hotel Emily was staying at, and some car just came out of nowhere."

"Did anyone see what happened?"

"I guess they have footage of the accident on the security cameras," she says.

"So they caught the person?"

She sucks in, and through sobs, she explains, "No, they were wearing sunglasses and a scarf, so they couldn't make out what they looked like. Oh, Nathan, it's all just too terrible. She was starting over, you know?"

"What about the car? Do they know the make of it?" I inquire.

I hear Michelle blow her nose before she answers. "I guess they found the car. It had been stolen, and whoever it was abandoned it. Isn't that terrible? Who would do something like that?"

"Is Lizzy going to be okay?"

"They don't know. The doctors put her in a coma because of her injuries. They said they wanted to give her body time to heal. But now that they have taken her off everything, she still hasn't woken up. It's my baby. What am I going to do?"

"Where is she?"

"She's in the ICU at Mass General."

"I'll be right there," I reply, not waiting for Michelle to answer before I hang up. I'm not thinking about anything except getting to Lizzy.

29

"Elizabeth Foster," I repeat for a third time, not hiding my aggravation. "She was brought in two weeks ago, a victim of a hit-and-run."

"Sir, do you even understand how many patients this hospital has at any given time?" The nurse is just as aggravated with me.

"Nathan?" I hear Savannah's voice behind me. I spin around wide-eyed.

"Oh my God, Savannah, hi, yes, will you please tell this woman that Liz is a patient here. She says they can't find her in the system."

"Sir, I'm sorry, but there is no Elizabeth Foster here," the woman says, glaring at me.

"She's right," Savannah confirms.

"What? No, her mom called me."

"She's under her maiden name now," Savannah says. I am in such a panic, it never crossed my mind that she was no longer Elizabeth Foster. I am not her husband, and she is not my wife.

I shake my head. "I'm such an idiot," I grumble.

Savannah smiles at the nurse. "I'll show him where to go."

The nurse doesn't reply, only squints at me as we move down the hallway.

"How is she?" I ask Savannah, hearing the panic in my voice.

"She got hit by a car. How do you think she is?" Savannah seems irritated, and I'm unsure what I did to warrant the reaction.

"I can't imagine what kind of monster could do this to someone," I say. Anger washes over me, and I'm furious that whoever did this is still out there, no consequences for what they did. Lizzy doesn't deserve it. "Her mom said she was at the parking garage of the hotel Emily was staying at. I assume Emily knows about this?"

"Of course she does." Savannah rolls her eyes in response to my question. "They were meeting with some associates of a friend of Liz's right before it happened."

"What?" I think of the powerful individual helping Liz, who Evelyn warned me about. "Are you talking about the people she mentioned at the storage locker?" I ask.

"Yeah," Savannah starts before she motions to a room. "She's in there."

I freeze. I'm not sure if I'm ready to see Liz in the state she's likely in. Savannah opens the door and then stops to look at me. "You coming or what?"

Before I enter, I hear the beeping of all the machines around her. My breath catches in my throat when I see the numerous tubes of fluid running in and out of various parts of Liz's body. Her face is bruised and swollen. Several limbs are in casts, but I can still see hints of the Liz from before.

"Are you fucking kidding me?" I cry as I race over to Liz's side. My phone vibrates in my pocket, but I ignore it. Nothing matters at the moment except Liz. I scoop up her hand and am careful how tight I hold it when I see the abrasions all over it. She looks broken, and it causes a physical response in me.

My head snaps in the direction of Savannah. "Are those assholes she was meeting with behind this?"

Savannah laughs before she crosses her arms. "Marla's crew? No way."

"Who's Marla?" I ask about the name I've never heard before.

"I don't see why that's any of your business," Savannah huffs.

"Because if she is behind this, I need to know to make sure Liz is safe from this happening again."

Savannah shakes her head. "Well, you don't have to worry about Marla. She's a friend Lizzy made on the inside."

"How do you know she didn't do this?" I demand, fixing my eyes back on Liz's battered face.

"Oh please, Marla is helping her. They are friends. She has zero reasons to hurt Liz. You know exactly who this was." Savannah snarls at me in disgust.

I glance back at her over my shoulder.

"You and I both know this was Evelyn."

I shake my head. "How would she know how to find Liz?" I can't argue that it wasn't her because as soon as Liz's mom said it was a hit-and-run, the thought that it could have been Evelyn crossed my mind. My phone starts to vibrate. I slip my phone out with my free hand and look at the caller ID. My stomach sinks. It's Evelyn. I should already be back with the boxes from the hardware store by now.

"Look, I know you care about Liz. I do too. I want to protect her." She rolls her eyes again when I speak.

"It looks like you're the one she needs protecting from," Savannah says through gritted teeth.

"That's not fair. I'm trying to help Liz."

"All I know is we talk to you at the storage facility, and the next thing I know, she's getting run down. How do I know you didn't go back and tell your wife everything, and that's why this happened? Maybe you're in on it with her."

"Shit," I gasp, my mouth falling open. Was this my fault? I confronted Evelyn. I revealed everything to her I was suspicious about. Had I set this into motion?

"What?"

I shake my head and look up at her. "Maybe you're right. Maybe this is my fault."

Savannah scoffs. "Well, I didn't expect that to come out of your mouth."

"I never thought she would do something like this," I say, my eyes fixed on Liz.

"Based on the information Marla called with a couple of days ago, there's a lot you probably don't realize about your wife."

"Wait, what?" My head snaps in her direction. "You heard from Liz's friend?"

She nods, pursing her lips before she says, "Once you know this, you can't un-know it."

"Fine, just tell me," I demand.

Savannah turns and walks over to a couple of chairs in the corner of the room, near the window. "You really should be sitting for this."

I move over to the chair next to her. I huff and plop down in the seat. "Now, will you tell me?"

"Are you sure you want to know?" she asks again, and I can see actual concern behind her eyes this time, but then it disappears.

What could she be so scared to tell me? Did these people find proof that Evelyn is keeping more secrets from me than I thought?

I nod, unable to bring myself to speak the affirmation.

Savannah looks at me, to Liz, and then back at me. "Okay, but I did warn you. These people who work with Marla, well, they do a lot of things that aren't exactly legal."

"That would explain why Liz met this woman while she was behind bars."

"Yeah, well, it ends up that word on the street is that a woman was willing to pay top dollar for a baby about twenty weeks ago." Savannah looks at me from under her brows, waiting for me to speak.

I shake my head. "Okay, and this has to do with Liz how?"

Savannah clears her throat. "The woman was insistent that she needed the baby right away, and she would pay extra if it was a newborn."

"That's terrible. I still don't see what this has to do with what happened to Liz," I say.

"I'm getting there. Hold your horses." She huffs. "Well,

it ends up they found a person willing to sell their baby, so they reached out to the woman to arrange the exchange. The only problem was, she said she already found one."

"You lost me."

"Emily reached out to a detective she used to know on the force when she covered the crime beat here in Boston. It ends up that around the same time this mysterious woman was on the hunt for a baby to buy, a homeless woman came into the hospital saying some woman stole her baby. They examined her, and she had just given birth hours before. The woman was a known addict, and the police assumed that the baby was probably already dead, and she was just whacked out of her mind."

"That's terrible, but I still don't understand what that has to do with what's happening."

"Your wife handles cases of women who are drug addicts and helps determine if they're a danger to their children sometimes, right?" As soon as Savannah poses the question, I start to shake my head.

"No, it can't be." The memory of the prosthetic stomach in the storage locker consumes my thoughts. Evelyn never wanted me at the doctor's visits. She refused to let me see her naked. Any glimpse I may have had of her stomach could have been the prosthetic. I recall how it felt like real skin when I touched it in the locker.

"Liz tried to tell you," Savannah states dismissively.

"I would have known, right?" I look up at Savannah, desperate for her to tell me this is a mistake. She shrugs.

I collapse back into the chair, sliding lower in my seat. "Evelyn was adamant that she wanted me to go to my friend's bachelor party. I was so upset when I got home and realized that she'd had the baby while I was gone. She didn't even call me."

"She's pure evil," Savannah gulps.

My phone buzzes again, and my stomach twists itself into knots before I look at the screen. I know it's her. "It's Evelyn. What do I do? The baby is at home with her. What if she tries to . . .?" I can't finish the statement.

"You have to answer," Savannah suggests. "Tell her everything's okay."

"What if she knows I'm here? She works here. She has friends that may have called her."

"I don't know, but you have to say something." Savannah is panicking as well.

"Evelyn?" I answer just before the call is shifted to voicemail.

"Where are you?" She sounds angry.

"Oh my God, Evelyn," I start. I decide the safest option I have is to tell her the truth, at least part of it. "I was on my way to get the boxes when Liz's mom called me."

"What? Why would she call you?"

"Liz was involved in a hit-and-run."

"Oh, babe, that's terrible," she says, and it makes my skin crawl. "That must be so hard for her mom to get her daughter back, only to lose her again."

"I know, right?" I decide it best not to tell Evelyn that Liz isn't gone.

"Are you with her mom now?" Evelyn inquires.

"Yeah, I'm sorry, I should have called. It just all happened so quickly." I lie about being with Michelle.

"No, I understand," Evelyn says.

"I'm going to head over and get those boxes, and then I'll be home, okay?" I assure her.

"Forget the boxes," she replies. "Just come home."

"Are you sure?"

"Yeah, we can deal with that later. I just want you here with us." If she was involved in what happened to Liz, I'm chilled to the bone by her response.

"Okay, I'll be home soon," I say before I hang up the phone.

Savannah gasps as if she had been holding her breath during the call. "What are you going to do?" she asks.

I take a deep breath. "I have no idea."

30

Anxiety tightens its grip on me, and I can't shake the feeling of dread as I drive home. The image of Lizzy's battered body is burned into my mind. Could Evelyn be capable of such a violent act? Is there a chance that Madison isn't mine? My eyes start to burn and grow wet at the idea. I can't go there. I can't allow myself to think of such an idea, but I also know this became much more complicated than something I can sort through. I need help. I place the call I know I have to. It repeatedly rings until the detective's voicemail picks up.

"Hello, it's Nathan Foster again. I need you to call me back as soon as you can." I state my phone number, though I'm confident the detective already has it, and hang up.

I'm on autopilot as I drive home, barely noticing my surroundings, wishing desperately the detective would return my call. My original conclusion about the prosthetic stomach being a therapy tool might be valid, but my gut tells me it's wishful thinking. If Madison isn't mine, how is it possible that I love her as much as I do? I was my father's biological child, and I never felt loved by the man. Clearly, biology has nothing to do with the affection one feels for a child.

While there's a chance it's all coincidence and there's nothing to the accusations, I have a hard time shaking off my doubt when I add all the things together. The lies Evelyn told about her father, the hidden storage unit, the articles about Patty Dane, the woman's missing baby, Lizzy's accident.

My heart aches when the accident enters my thoughts again. I can still hear the machines beeping and buzzing around her—my anguish shifts to anger, then my phone rings.

"Hello?" I say, picking up the call.

"Mr. Foster, hello, I was just returning your call. It's Detecti—"

"Detective, yes, hello," I interrupt him. "Thank you so much for calling me back."

"Your message seemed urgent," he says.

"It is," I begin, trying not to think about what the aftermath of this conversation will look like. "Some things have come to my attention recently, and as crazy as it sounds, there's a chance that my wife might have been involved in Alison's death."

"Mr. Foster, I never hid the fact that I believe Elizabeth was behind the murder. You're not exactly offering me some shocking revelation here. Unless you have some new evidence to provide me with, I don't understand the point of your call."

"No," I correct him. "My current wife."

"What?"

"Yes, Dr. Evelyn Powell, well, Foster now."

"I don't understand. Did your current wife know the victim?"

"I'm not sure, but there's a chance she may have." I sigh as I prepare to reveal all the details I have uncovered about Evelyn. "I know this sounds crazy, but please, hear me out," I plead. I tell him everything. How Evelyn went to see Liz in prison, and what Liz claimed that Evelyn confessed to her. I explain about the key to the storage locker Evelyn hid. The articles I found and then how everything disappeared.

After everything, I add, "I also think there's a chance Evelyn may have been involved in a recent attempt on Liz's life."

"Someone tried to kill your ex-wife?"

"Yes, she was the victim of a hit-and-run," I explain.

"And is your new wife aware of everything you think about her?"

"She knows something, but I'm not sure how much."

"You understand how far-fetched this all sounds, don't you?" the detective asks.

"Of course I do, but I can't keep ignoring everything. I don't know how Evelyn found me or how Patty came across Alison, but somehow, it's all connected. I'm certain of it now."

I don't tell him about my suspicions that Madison isn't mine. I'm not sure if it's because I am worried she will be taken away from me or if I'm not yet convinced of that part of the story.

"Well?" I ask after a moment of lingering silence.

"Mr. Foster, I have always thought Liz was guilty of the murder of that poor woman, but I'll admit, it's quite a compelling detail that your new wife used to be Patty Dane's doctor."

"What do I do?"

"Until I have a chance to look into this and confirm the facts, nothing. It would probably be best for you and your daughter if Evelyn is unaware of what you're thinking."

"And I'm just supposed to what? Act like everything is fine and go to bed next to this woman who could be a killer?"

"I can't advise you what you should do when it comes to your wife, sir." The detective sounds annoyed again.

I pull into the parking spot next to Evelyn's car. "Yeah, well, thanks for nothing." I hang up the phone, no closer to figuring out what I should do next.

I enter the elevator and press the button to our floor. It feels like I'm on a death march. What if Evelyn is precisely who I fear she is, and she knows everything? The moment I step foot into our condo, it could all be over. What other options do I have? My daughter is in there, and she needs me. I place one foot in front of the other and remind myself I'm the only father she has.

31

E velyn is sitting at the kitchen table, staring down the hall at the front door as I enter. Her hair is smooth and looks as though she recently brushed it. She seems calm, and I'm unsure if I should feel reassured or terrified by that. As I enter the home, all the lights are off except the under-counter lights in the kitchen, and there's an orange glow coming from the fireplace in the living room. In the background, I hear music playing softly.

"Hi," Evelyn says, watching me as I walk into the room. There is no way to get a read on her expression in the darkness. "How's Liz's mom doing?"

I shrug. "As well as one would expect, I suppose."

As I move farther into the room, my attention shifts to the stove and the whistling of a teapot.

"That's terrible. Her family must be so upset. Do they know what happened?" Evelyn stands and moves over to the teapot, removing it from the flame. I glance around the living room and don't see Madison. I feel a slight twinge of panic in my gut.

I shake my head. "Some random hit-and-run, I guess."

"I guess you were right. We do live in such a scary world, don't we?" she says before asking if I would like a cup of tea.

Act normal. What would I usually do? "Sure," I reply, taking a seat at the dining room table as she retrieves two mugs from the cabinet. "Where's Madison?"

She smiles as she approaches me. "Where do you think she is?" She laughs. "She's in her crib, silly."

"Oh, of course. I guess I didn't realize how late it was."

"I was very worried about you," she continues as she pours the hot water over the tea bags.

"I'm sorry I didn't call you," I quickly add. "Liz's mom called me, and then everything was just so crazy after that."

"No, I completely understand," she says, setting the mug of tea in front of me. "Liz was your wife for a very long time. I'm sure this must all feel very confusing for you."

She isn't wrong. When I saw Lizzy in that hospital bed, I felt rage for her pain and the urge to protect her. The idea it could have been inflicted on her by my now wife makes me even angrier. The detective is aware of her involvement now. There's a chance I'll have the answers I crave very soon.

The way I reacted when I heard about Lizzy being in the hospital. The feelings that came over me when I saw her in the bed, made it clear I'm not over her. If it's apparent to me, I wonder if Evelyn can tell the same when she looks at me. Can she see how torn up I am about Liz's accident? Does it make her feel betrayed? What is she capable of if she thinks I betrayed her?

Evelyn pulls out the tea bag and stirs a teaspoon of honey into my glass. She remembers things about me, like the way I like my tea. I may have overlooked her being a psychopath. She's better at pretending than I am.

I watch as she takes a sip from her mug. I realize I'm staring at her when she asks, "What? Do I have something on my face?"

"No." I shake my head and chuckle. I need to keep her disarmed. She needs to believe that nothing is wrong. "I was just thinking how lucky I am to be with someone as understanding as you."

She offers me a tight-lipped grin before she takes another sip of her tea. I take a drink of mine. "You're so sweet, babe," she says at last. "I'm looking forward to moving to Michigan with you. Everything is going to be better when we get there."

"Yeah." I shrug, taking another sip of my tea.

She continues to watch me quietly.

I yawn. "Oh my God, I can't believe how tired I am all of a sudden. I feel like I didn't get very much done today."

Evelyn sighs and slumps back into her chair.

"Is something wrong?" I ask.

She scoffs. "No, just thinking of something my therapist once told me."

"Your therapist?" I ask, surprised. I hadn't known Evelyn was in therapy, and I wonder if this is someone she's seeing now or if it was before me.

She nods. "I never understood when she used to ask

me why I can't let myself be happy, that is, until I met you. We're exactly alike in that way."

"Ouch," I say, half-joking, yawning again.

"I guess Evelyn did know what she was talking about," she says.

I blink at her repeatedly, trying to make sense of what she just said, but it's like her words are drowning in static. "Evelyn?" I manage at last.

She sighs. "I kept telling you Liz was going to try to ruin everything, but you couldn't see it. I don't blame you. You're too close to the situation to see it as clearly as I can."

"Wh-what are you talking about?" My voice sounds low, and the words slowly drag out of me.

"You were going to leave me," she says pointedly.

"No, I'm not."

She shakes her head, then crosses her arms. "It's okay. I was here before. I know what it looks like when someone is going to leave. Evelyn was going to leave me too."

"What are you saying?" My head feels like it's too heavy to hold upright anymore, and I let it rest on one of my shoulders. I try to concentrate on Evelyn's face, but it keeps going in and out of focus.

"You know, I didn't lie about everything. Of course, you believe everything that Liz tells you. My dad abused me, and he is dead. I know because I killed him. Evelyn helped me see that it wasn't my fault. I was driven to it. What I did was because of all the years of abuse I'd suffered at his hands. She saw me in a way nobody else ever had. I wasn't a monster. I was the victim. And just when I finally thought I found someone who cared about me and would never hurt me the way my father had, she told me she was moving to Boston. She said she couldn't be my doctor anymore. I couldn't allow that."

"Patty." The name slips off my lips as my blinks slow.

"I didn't mean to hurt her. I loved her. I was trying to get her to listen, and she hit her head. It wasn't my fault. It was an accident. That's when I realized what Evelyn had done for me. She made the ultimate sacrifice for my happiness. So I got rid of her body, and I burned the place down." She giggles and bobs her head. "Well, I suppose that's a little dramatic. It was just one wing that burned."

"You . . . Evelyn's identity?" I can't form complete sentences anymore.

"Did I steal Evelyn's identity?" she asks, lifting her brows. "It's not like she was going to use it anymore."

"Madis—"

"I told you, Madison is just fine. She's sleeping, and very soon, you will be too." I try to stand but realize I can't even lift a hand. The tea. Or was it the honey?

"I don't blame you. You're as much a victim of Liz as I was a victim of my father. She knows how to manipulate you. When I saw her at the restaurant, I told her I would kill her if she ever came near you again. She didn't listen to me, so I had to do it. You can understand that, right? But apparently, I still have to finish the job."

"Please," I say in a whisper. In my mind, I'm telling her we can leave, there's no reason for her to hurt anyone else, but my brain can't seem to make my mouth say the words.

"Do you think I'm that stupid? I could hear the hospital pages when I was on the phone with you. As soon as you hung up, I called and figured out Liz was still alive."

A static of panic shoots out from my core, and I feel it in my fingertips, but I still can't budge my limbs. I wonder if Evelyn drugged Alison before she killed her. Part of me hopes she did. I hate the thought of her in pain or being as scared as I feel right now.

I feel a dull sensation as Patty's hand falls on my cheek after she stands. She's hovering over me, caressing my face, and I'm helpless, unable to recoil at her touch.

"Don't worry. I know how to fix this. I realize now we can't be together as a family until Liz is gone, really gone. I'm going to take care of this, and when I get back, we can go to Michigan and leave all of this in the past, where it belongs." Desperation grips me as my eyes close, and Evelyn's—Patty's—words fade into the darkness that swallows me.

32

I wake surrounded by darkness. My head is pounding, and my mouth is dry. I question if my eyes are open, and that's when I see a sliver of light peeking out from under the door. I reach around frantically, trying to figure out where I am.

Damn it, why does my head hurt so bad?

My hand settles on an item . . . a cereal box, my other hand on a can of some kind. I'm in the pantry. It's small and cramped, and I have trouble standing but eventually make my way upright and reach out for the door handle. When I finally find it and twist, panic explodes inside me when it won't turn completely. I throw my body into the door, but it doesn't budge. Something must be wedged against the outside.

Patty! I close my eyes and try to remember everything that led to me waking up in the pantry. Through my pounding head, I remember the startling revelation. The woman I married is not Evelyn Powell. She is Patty Dane.

She drugged me. What did she say to me before I passed out?

Shaking, the memory comes to me. She's planning to kill Liz. I try the handle again, desperate to free myself from the prison Patty locked me in. My thoughts shift from Liz to Madison. She said Madison was sleeping. I have to get out of here to make sure she's okay.

"Patty! Are you out there?" I shout. "Please, you have to let me out of here. I'm not mad. We can talk about it. Please, just let me out."

I wait, listening with my ear pressed to the door. There is music playing in the background, but I can't hear anything else.

"Help!" I shout as loud as possible, but it will take time, even if someone hears me. They'll call the police, then the police will search the place before they find me. I have to figure a way out of here. Liz and Madison need me now.

I check my pockets. She took my phone.

I fumble around for the light above my head. It is usually controlled by motion sensors, but Patty must have turned the manual switch off. I find and flip the switch, letting out a moan as the sudden and blinding light sends pain piercing through my brain.

When my eyes adjust, I look for anything that might help me out of the small space. I try the handle again, then throw my weight against the door repeatedly.

"Damn it!" I shout, throwing my head up in frustration. My breath catches in my throat when I see the small access hatch in the ceiling. I desperately search for something to stand on but don't find anything. I put my weight on one of the shelves, but it immediately begins to pull away from the wall.

I jump for the hatch, my fingertips causing the panel to dislodge. My head jerks wildly, looking for anything to give me a few more inches. That's when I catch sight of the extra diapers and formula I'd recently purchased on the floor at the back of the closet. I place the diapers on the stacked formula cans and leap for the access hatch. The panel covering the opening moves to one side. It takes me a few tries of re-stacking the toppling tower before I'm able to grab the edges of the opening and pull myself up. The space is short, and ductwork is weaved throughout the beams.

In the distance, I can see a sliver of light beaming up from below and realize it must be another access point. Carefully, I crawl through the pitch-black maze, trying to keep my weight on the cross beams by feeling, as I cannot see them. When I finally reach the light source, I pull off the panel and drop down, prepared to attack if I must. I'm in Madison's closet and see an open box of her clothes on the floor. I look up, the closet door is open, and I can see her crib. As silently as I can, I tiptoe to the crib, prepared to grab Madison and run out of the condo.

My chest tightens when I reach the crib, and it's empty. I look around for something I can use as a weapon, but most things have been packed. I grab a potted plant from the window ledge and decide it will have to do. I hold my breath with determination and stealthiness, searching the condo for any trace of Patty or Madison. Neither one is anywhere to be found.

That's when it hits me. Liz. I have no phone to call. I

search for my keys, but they are gone as well. I run to the table in the hallway, but my spare set isn't there. She's going to kill Liz.

I'm barefoot, but I have no time for shoes. I run out the front door and start pounding on my neighbor's door, then the next and the next until finally, one of the first doors I was banging on opens.

I recognize the woman but don't remember her name. She's an older lady, and I know from talk around the building that her husband passed away last year. She's the one I always see in the elevator with her bag of knitting materials.

"Mr. Foster?" I feel bad when I realize she knows my name and I don't remember hers.

I run back and face her. She looks down at my bare feet. "I need you to call the police," I exclaim.

"What's wrong?" She grips the edge of the door, and I can tell that I'm scaring her.

"Someone broke into my house and stole my car keys and my phone." The situation isn't one that I can easily or quickly explain. If I try to, I'm confident I will sound crazy.

"Oh no." She takes a couple of steps back. "Are they still in the building?"

"No, I don't think so, but I did hear one of them say they were going to go to Mass General to kill a woman."

She blinks at me repeatedly, confused by my statement. "Mr. Foster, where are your wife and child?"

"They weren't home when it happened, thank goodness," I say. "Now, can you call the police and tell them they're heading to Mass General?"

"They broke in your house and said that right in front of you?"

"Yes!" I exclaim in frustration. "I know it sounds crazy, but please, I need your help. They took my phone, and I'm worried about my wife and daughter."

"Would you like to use my phone?" she offers.

"No, I need you to call the police as I asked. My wife works at the hospital, and I would feel much better if I could check on her in person. I hate to ask this but is there any way I can borrow a car?"

"What?" She closes the door a little between us. "I don't—"

"I know, it sounds crazy, but I'm your neighbor, so you know I'll return it. I need to go find my wife and daughter."

"I said you could call her."

"I'd feel better if I go and make sure they're safe. I'm sure you understand," I beg. I can tell that she doesn't trust me, and part of my story doesn't make sense to her, but she appears to be considering my request.

"Wait one minute," she says and closes the door. Time is slipping away from me. I have no idea where Patty is. For all I know, she may already be at the hospital, and Liz could already be dead. If that's the case, would she run? Would she take Madison with her?

The door opens, and my neighbor stands there with a set of car keys in one hand and her phone in the other.

"It was my Henry's," she says, handing the keys over to me. "Please be careful with it."

"I will," I assure her, turning toward the elevator, thankful for the kindness of a woman I barely know.

As I wait for the elevator doors to open, I hear her voice again. "Yes, hello, police, this is Alice McGowan. I live at—" Before I can hear more, I'm in the elevator and headed to the parking garage. Alice, I think to myself as I wait impatiently. I need to remember her name, and if I can save Liz, I need to make sure I tell Alice she saved someone's life tonight by trusting me.

When the elevator reaches the parking garage, I race to the numbered spots and find Henry McGowan's Lincoln sitting there. I waste no time jumping in and heading in the direction of the hospital. I'm not the type to pray, but all the way there, all I can do is ask God to keep Liz and Madison safe. I bargain with everything I have in the world if he will find a way to keep them safe. I will be a better man.

33

I throw the car into park at the hospital entrance, despite several angry paramedics yelling that I can't leave my car there. I don't have time, though. I also don't have time to explain the situation to all the nurses yelling at me as I'm racing down the hospital's hallways. I burst into the stairwell and start taking the steps two at a time until I reach the ICU floor.

My brain has trouble separating what all the different sounds are as I move in the direction of Liz's room. That's when I make out screaming and a commotion.

My legs burn after the stairs, but I fight through it as I get closer to Liz's room. I do not see any officers in the hallway. I should have told Alice a name to give the police. Mass General is massive. There is no way they would know where to begin. I hope my mistake doesn't get Liz killed.

Loud pops cut through the chaos, and I stop. I can't move. I know what the noise is without entering the room. I'm too late. Patty has taken Liz from me.

Every mistake I made that led to this moment settles over me. On the other side of the wall, the woman I love is dead or dying. "Liz," I cry before I fall to my knees. I can't bring myself to walk into the room. I hear one of the nurses behind me calling the police. I watch the doorway for Patty to leave. At that moment, my mind is made up. I'm going to kill her. I'm going to rid the world of her, not thinking it will leave Madison without either parent. I'm only thinking revenge.

I don't just want revenge on her for taking Liz from me. I want revenge for what she did to Alison and our unborn child. I want to punish her for the hell she put Liz through. So much of it was my fault; I see that now. I was weak. I was the one who cheated on my wife and gave this monster an opening to enter our lives. No more, though. The people I care about deserve justice. There is no way I will let her get away with it. If I couldn't protect Liz, I will avenge her. I grip the wall and pull myself upright, preparing to strangle the life out of the woman who stole everything from me.

"I mean it, get away from her." I hear a voice screaming. It's not Patty's, though. I recognize the voice. When I stumble in through the door, I see Liz's mother, Michelle, standing there, holding a gun. My eyes move to Liz, still asleep in the bed, monitors beeping wildly. Patty Dane is standing next to her with a knife in her hand. My instinct is to run at Patty and do whatever I have to to get her away from Liz, but then I think of Madison.

"Patty," I say in a sharp voice. I can see Michelle's head jerk in my direction from the corner of my eye.

"Nathan, she was going to kill her," Michelle cries, her hands trembling as they grip tightly to the gun in them.

I notice broken pieces of ceiling tile on the floor and realize the pops I heard must have only been warning shots.

"You just couldn't help yourself, could you?" Patty snarls as she glares at me.

"You don't need to do this," I say as I lift my hands in the air and start to inch closer to Patty. Reactively she extends her arm, placing the blade against Lizzy's throat.

Michelle gasps before she yells, "Get away from her, you psycho!"

Patty doesn't care that Michelle has a gun pointed at her; she never removes her eyes from my face.

"Ev, where's Madison?" I ask, desperation dripping from every word.

"Why did you have to follow me? You didn't have to see this," Patty says, pressing the knife harder against Lizzy's throat.

"I mean it; I'll shoot if you don't get away from her!" Michelle shouts.

From behind us, I hear a nurse yell, "She has a gun." Chaos erupts in the hallway, and I can see Patty's eyes start to dart back and forth from the door to me.

"There's no way you can get out of here if you hurt her," I say in a calm voice. "Why don't you put the knife down, and then you and I can go get Madison."

She shakes her head wildly. "I didn't do all this just to lose my family."

My heart is pounding, and I have to fight the urge to

leap for the knife. I'm uncertain if I can get there in time, and I can't risk Lizzy getting hurt.

"You don't have to," I lie. "We can walk out of here together. We'll head straight for Michigan. You haven't done anything yet that you can't undo."

"Are you insane?" Michelle gasps.

I wave a hand in her direction, never taking my eyes off of Patty.

"I'm not stupid," Patty hisses at me.

"I know," I say in a soft voice, inching slightly closer. "Patty, I've never had anyone love me as much as you do."

"I do love you," she repeats, and I see her relax her arm holding the knife. It's still close to Lizzy's throat but no longer pressed against it. "I would do anything for you and Madison."

"If that's true, then put the knife down," I state.

She shakes her head again. "I can't. You still love her."

"I do, you're right, but not the way I love you and Madison. I tried to make things work with Lizzy, but it just wasn't meant to be. You're my family now." As I say the words, I feel my stomach twist, and I hope I'm convincing.

"You're just saying what you think I want to hear," Patty replies.

"No, you're wrong. Why do you think I rushed all the way here? I wanted to stop you before you did something that would take you away from Madison and me forever. If you hurt Liz, they'll arrest you." I'm certain Patty has committed enough crimes that there is no doubt she's heading to prison. I only need to convince her that I believe it can be a new start for us if she leaves with me.

"You really want to be with me after—after all of this?"

"I'm not going to lie; it won't be easy," I reply. "But you gave me Madison, and there's nothing I want more than the three of us to be a family. Where's Madison, Patty? Can you take me to her?"

Patty looks down at Liz and then back to me. I hear chatter from the hallway and realize the police have arrived. I'm running out of time. If Patty feels threatened, there is no telling how she will react.

"Will you come with me?" I ask, extending a hand.

Patty swallows hard as her eyes fix themselves on my open hand. "I really did love you," she says in a quiet voice. "But I know you will never really be able to love me as long as Liz is still breathing."

Patty turns toward Liz and lifts the knife into the air, ready to bring it down into Lizzy's torso. I prepare to launch myself across the room when I hear several loud pops. I freeze, my eyes shifting to Michelle, a plume of smoke coming out from the end of the gun in her hands.

I look back at Patty, who is now slumped over Lizzy. Blood is starting to pool around the two of them on the bed.

"Liz!" I cry as I race over and pull Patty off. Patty's struggling to breathe as she whispers my name. I shift her to the side, trying to make sure none of the blood on the bed belongs to Liz.

"I don't think Liz is hurt," I say, trying to reassure Michelle.

"She was going to kill her, Nathan!" Michelle shrieks, the gun still gripped tightly in her hands.

"I know," I say, returning my attention to Patty. She

stares up at me, and she's scared. I hate that I feel bad for her. Moments ago, I wanted to kill her, to use my bare hands to strangle the life out of her.

"I shot her. I shot her."

"Michelle, I know!" I shout, glancing over at Michelle just as an officer comes up behind my ex-mother-in-law and takes the gun from her hands. A set of nurses rush forward through the door and start assessing the situation of both Liz and Patty. I hear one of them say they need to prep an operating room right away.

"Patty," I say, trying to keep her focus on me. "Where's Madison, Patty?"

She coughs, and blood sprays from her mouth.

"Sir, you need to step away," one of the nurses says as she pulls Patty from my grasp.

"The baby, where's the baby?" I shout as they load her onto a gurney.

Her eyes are still fixed on me. "We could have been a family," I hear her murmur. "We could have been happy." Her words are mixed with the sound of blood gurgling in her throat.

"Please, the baby." I'm desperate, but her eyes close with no other words.

"She's crashing." I hear one of the nurses say as they wheel her out of the room and down the hall.

I step back as a circle of nurses surrounds Lizzy. I see one of them retrieve the knife Patty had been wielding. She delivers it to another officer that has just entered the room, along with an explanation I can't hear.

The new officer's eyes lock onto me. She is staring at my chest. I look down to see I'm covered in Patty's blood. I hear Michelle's sobbing start to grow louder as the first officer helps her to a chair off to the side.

I look back at the female officer who's still staring at me. She's now standing right in front of me. I look at the knife she's holding. The blade that Patty was prepared to thrust into Lizzy just minutes ago. I start to breathe a little easier as the reality settles over me that Lizzy is safe. And just as quickly as that calm came to me, it disappears as my thoughts shift to Madison.

"Can you tell me what happened here?" the officer asks.

"My daughter," I gasp. "She's missing. That woman they just wheeled out of here took her, and I don't know what she did with her."

"What do you mean she took her?"

"I mean, she took her, and now she's gone!" I'm shouting, and the officer is uneasy in response.

"How old is your daughter, sir?"

"She's just a baby, five months," I answer.

"Do you have a description of what she was wearing?" the officer asks.

"Wearing? No! She's a baby!" I feel like a shitty father. How do I not know what she's wearing? How can I call myself her father when I can't protect her?

"Sir, I need you to calm down," the officer warns. I see from the corner of my eye they're handcuffing Michelle.

"Hey, what are you doing? You can't do that." I race over to assist Liz's mother when the female officer twists my arm, and swipes a foot under my legs, causing me to fall forward.

"We're taking her in for further questioning," the officer who placed the cuffs on her says.

I'm disoriented; I realize the female officer is also placing me in handcuffs. "What are you doing?" I cry. "I didn't do anything."

"Then you have nothing to worry about," she replies. "But until we figure out what happened here, we need everyone involved to come along with us."

As she helps me stand, I argue that she has to let me go because I have to find my daughter. She assures me they have every officer in the area searching for her.

"Madison needs me," I plead. "You have to find her."

They guide Michelle and me toward a waiting squad car, and the memory of the night Liz was arrested comes to my mind. Michelle is no longer crying. She's fallen into some sort of trance and is staring into nothingness. The only evidence of what happened is the tear-stained mascara trail on her cheeks and the handcuffs on her wrists.

I continue pleading with the officers that they have to let me help look for Madison or at least let me stay there until they find her, but the officer ignores me. When we're in the car, waiting for the driver to get in, I hear an announcement over the radio.

First, the word baby jumps out at me, and then something else that I can't hear. The original officer that placed me in handcuffs opens my door and looks at me.

"I believe we found your daughter—"

"Is she okay?" I interrupt.

She nods. "It appears so. Does your daughter have a puffy pink coat with butterflies on it?"

I nod. "Yes," I gasp in relief. "It's lined in white fur."

"An officer found her asleep in a car seat in one of the cars in the parking lot."

"Oh, thank God," I groan as a flood of tears breaks free.

"We'll have someone from social services take her to the precinct."

Liz and Madison are safe. For the first time this evening, I'm able to breathe.

34

"You ready? You sure you don't want my help?" I ask, fighting the urge to take Liz's arm.

"I told you I want to do this on my own," she says, gripping the edges of the wheelchair as she judges the distance with her eyes from the chair to the car.

"Oh, will you just let him help you already?" Michelle huffs, standing next to the passenger door.

Liz glares at her mother, and it's strangely comforting to see that their relationship is starting to return to normal. It didn't take long for the police to review the evidence against Patty and determine Michelle was acting in defense of herself and her daughter when she shot Patty.

Emily and I were the first two faces Liz saw when she woke up. Both Michelle and Savannah were annoyed they'd missed the moment while grabbing lunch together. Emily and Savannah are still not big fans of mine, but Michelle and I have managed to find a connection we never had when I was her son-in-law.

I hover behind Liz as she pulls herself into the back seat. She's right. She's just fine on her own. I close her door, wheel the chair back to the hospital entrance, and get in the driver's side.

"How ya doing?" I ask, glancing in my rearview mirror.

"Just watch the potholes," she laughs.

"You got it," I reply.

"I still don't understand why you can't stay with us," Michelle chimes.

"Mom, I don't want to go through this again," Liz groans.

"I'm your mother. I should be the one taking care of you."

"I told you, Emily is moving back with her son and fiancé, and I'm going to stay with them while I'm doing rehab. Their rental is much closer to the hospital than your place; it makes sense."

"I said I would drive you," Michelle replies, glancing over at me.

"Mom," Liz huffs.

"I appreciate you letting me drive her, Michelle. It's nice to be able to do something for her."

"Mm-hmm," she grunts in response.

"Mom said you went to see Madison on your way here today," Lizzy interjects, and I can tell she's trying to put an end to her mother's scrutiny.

"I did," I exclaim as I pull out of the parking lot in the direction of Emily's new place.

After Patty died, I could have stayed silent. Nobody would question if Madison was my biological child or not. In the end, though, I would never be able to live with myself if I didn't have a DNA test done. I thought of Liz, and the way losing Matthew broke her. If there was a chance Madison wasn't mine, I had to make sure. I was heartbroken when the results revealed she was not my biological daughter. After some investigative work on Emily and her detective friend's part, it was confirmed that Patty kidnapped her from one of her patients who was living on the streets.

"Has her mother decided what she's going to do?" Liz inquires.

"She felt she wasn't in the best place to be a mother after all, so it sounds like she asked her mom to take her," I explain, trying to hide how sad it makes me that I'm not going to be the person Madison wakes to see every morning.

"When are you supposed to have the meeting with your attorney about custody?" Liz asks.

Michelle starts to fidget with the hem of her shirt. Everything about Patty makes her feel uncomfortable, including discussing the child I once thought I shared with her. I can only imagine what it must feel like for her to be the one to have taken Patty's life. I'm sure it leaves a stain that is hard to wash away, though I'm thankful she did it because it means Liz is still here, part of my life again in some small way, even if it's just as friends.

"I already did," I say.

"What? I didn't know that." Liz sounds surprised.

"Yeah, it doesn't look good." I nod. I don't say anything; I don't want to ruin the mood of the day. Liz is getting out of the hospital, and we should be celebrating.

"I don't understand. You're the only father she's ever known."

"I agree, but according to my attorney, even though I didn't know she was kidnapped, I have no legal right to her." I know Maddie won't remember me, though it hurts too much to admit that out loud.

"You would be the best father she could ever hope for," Liz adds.

I smile at her in the mirror before readjusting my eyes to the road. "Thank you." The truth is I'd give anything to be Madison's father, but as much as I want custody of her, I can understand where social services is coming from. I want Madison to feel safe and loved. If she learns that my wife kidnapped her, how can she not feel betrayed? If her mother isn't up to the task, it's probably still in Madison's best interest that someone in her family cares for her. Even though I want to be in her life more than anything else, I always want her to feel safe.

The most important lesson I learned in my short time of being a father is it's not about you or what you want; it's about what's best for your child. Madison may never know how much I love her. There's a good chance at some point her family will no longer want me to be a part of her life, so I have to accept what will be best for her.

"I'm so sorry," Liz says. She knows more than anyone what I'm going through. We lost Matthew. The pain of losing a child is a sting that never goes away.

"Thank you," I reply, turning my attention to her mother. "So, how are you doing with everything, Michelle?"

"What's that supposed to mean?" She huffs as she crosses her arms.

Liz shakes her head and rolls her eyes. "He wants to know how you're dealing with being a killer, Mom."

"You're not funny, Elizabeth," Michelle snaps.

"It must have been terrible for you when your church group heard what you did," Liz adds mockingly.

"I mean it, young lady, I do not think you're funny, not one bit."

Liz laughs. "Uh-oh, I better watch myself. She's pulling the young lady on me."

"Come on, Lizzy, take it easy on her," I say with a chuckle. "She did save your life after all."

"At least someone in this car appreciates me," Michelle whines.

"I'm sorry, Mom. I was being a jerk," Liz says with a hint of sarcasm.

Michelle shrugs her shoulders, but I can tell she appreciates the apology, even with the sarcasm. "I'm just glad that awful woman can't hurt anyone else ever again. Did you two see the story on the news where they interviewed Evelyn's parents?"

"No, I missed that one," I answer. The truth is I got rid of every television in my place. I can't handle another media circus. Once the press got ahold of the latest in our story, I knew it would be relentless. My friend Travis rented a place for me in his name in hopes that the press won't be able to figure out where I live. So far, so good.

"It's just awful," Michelle continues. "All this time, they thought their daughter hated them and wanted nothing to do with them and then to find out she was murdered. And what's worse, they still don't know what that woman did with her body. I can't imagine what they are going through."

"I packed up the letters I found from the family in her office and mailed them back to them," I say.

"What did you say?" Michelle asks, her mouth gaping open as she awaits my reply.

"Nothing, I just put them in a box and shipped them off. I felt like they should have them back."

"It's crazy to think you were sleeping right next to her and never knew."

"Mom!" Liz scolds from the back seat.

"What?" she hisses. "I'm just saying."

"Well, stop," Liz commands.

"Patty destroyed a lot of families with what she did," I state.

"I almost wish she was still alive so she could face trial," Michelle adds. "Did you know some people are still saying that Elizabeth killed Alison?"

"Mom, only the nut job conspiracy theorists say that," Liz groans.

"Say what you will, but people are still saying it," Michelle adds.

"And some people still say the earth is flat, and we never landed on the moon," Liz grumbles as she crosses her arms and looks out the window.

"Well, I think this will all eventually blow over," I offer as I pull into the driveway of Emily's rental property. She's standing with her son, waiting for us to arrive. It's a testament to Liz that there are people fighting over the privilege to take care of her.

. . .

I HELP Liz into the house and tell her I'll stop in and see how she's doing. There's so much commotion, I'm not sure she hears me. But it's best to sneak away quietly and allow her this time with her friends and family. I'm no longer that; I'm part of her past.

35

SIX MONTHS LATER

I watch each face as they enter the coffee shop. I wonder if I will recognize Liz when I see her. There were so many times over the last six months I wanted to visit her, but it never felt like an appropriate time. She was busy with physical therapy, and when she wasn't there, Emily was with her. I don't feel like I belong. I brought Patty into our lives, maybe indirectly, but her obsession with me and my affair with Alison gave her opportunity.

I started therapy after the incident at the hospital. Initially, my lawyer said it would help my custody bid for Madison and show I was working through all the trauma I went through. After dropping the custody case, I continued the sessions. They helped me see I claimed too much responsibility for what happened.

Maybe Patty would have still latched onto our scent that day she noticed us at the hospital, the day we lost Matthew, but I kept telling myself it was my infidelity that pushed Lizzy to the brink in the first place. It was my relationship with Alison that got her killed. Patty's desperation to hold on to me was behind kidnapping Madison. All the people I cared about were hurt by the choices I made.

In therapy, we're exploring my selfish behaviors and how, while they are deserving of consequences, they are separate and not linked to the responsibility of what Patty did. The guilt for those crimes is solely on her. By carrying them on my shoulders, I choose to continue to be her victim. The funny thing is that Patty's own words helped me understand what I was doing. She once told me my father only had the control over me that I allowed him to have. I'd done the same thing with her, and I finally realized I gave Patty enough of my life.

Liz walks in the door, and any doubt I have that I might not recognize her bleeds away. Her hair is long again, like it was when we were married. She is back at a fuller weight, and she looks more familiar to me—good, healthy. I wave a hand in her direction.

Her eyes light up when she sees me. There are no bruises, no casts. She's walking as if nothing ever happened. It isn't until she approaches the table that I see the scar along her cheek, a pink and white reminder of the hell she's been through. It doesn't diminish her beauty at all. Instead, I think about how strong she looks with it.

I'm standing. We smile awkwardly at each other.

"Hey, sorry I'm late," she says.

"I got you a pumpkin spice latte," I say, pointing at the cup in front of me.

"Oh lord, is it already that time of year again?" She

laughs as she asks the question, taking a seat and sipping the drink.

"Are you kidding? You used to be the first one in line every year on the first day they were in season."

She shrugs. "It just doesn't seem as important anymore, I guess."

She is right. We both went through so much. Much more than anyone should have to go through in their lifetime. Many of the things that used to matter no longer do.

I chuckle. "You know, my therapist says something similar. After what we went through, it changes your priorities."

"Whoa, back up," Lizzy says, holding up a hand. "Did I just hear Nathan Foster say he is in therapy?"

I smile. "Well, yes, there's a lot about me you probably are unaware of these days."

"Oh, now I'm intrigued," she smiles. I miss her smile. "Do tell."

"You promise not to make fun of me?"

She squints at me. "Since I don't know what you're going to say, how about I promise to try not to?"

I laugh. "Fine, laugh if you must. In addition to therapy, I'm taking some classes on self-awareness, and I sit in on a couple group grief sessions every week."

"Get out! I don't believe my ears."

"I'm serious. If it wasn't for all that, I don't think I'd be a functioning human right now," I admit.

She nods and offers me a tender smile. "I get it. I started seeing a therapist that specializes in trauma," she says. "But what's been my biggest help is working at the prison."

I repeatedly blink, a little surprised by the news. "When did this happen?"

"A few months ago."

"I would've thought you'd never want to set foot in that place again," I say.

"I would've said you were right if you'd asked me before everything with Patty happened, but something changed when she was gone. It wasn't just about revenge or trying to prove I didn't do what everyone thought I did. There was no more fight left for me to win, so I had to figure out what really made me want to get up in the morning."

"And that was working at the prison?" I can't help but laugh a little when I ask the question.

"I know it probably doesn't make sense to you, but I met a lot of amazing women there. So many of them are victims of circumstance. They aren't terrible people; they were dealt a shitty hand in life. I think they need someone who's seen it from the same perspective. It can feel pretty hopeless when you're in there."

"That's amazing, Liz; what are you doing there?"

"I'm teaching a creative writing class and a class on how to write a résumé." She's beaming with pride. "It's not a ton of time, but I love it."

"I'm so damn proud of you."

"Thanks, I'm pretty proud of myself too." She smiles before she takes another sip of her coffee. "So what about you? How's your job going?"

"What job?" I ask, lifting my brows.

"You didn't go back to the firm?" She seems surprised, and I like that I can create that reaction in her.

I shake my head. "I couldn't see going back after everything that happened. I thought I'd figure out what the next chapter in my life would look like pretty quickly, but I don't think I'm any closer to figuring out what I want to do than when I started."

"How's your dad feel about that?"

"I wouldn't know," I say, stiffening at the thought of the man I used to let control so many aspects of my life.

"Really?"

"I wish I'd cut him out of my life while we were together," I admit.

"I know more than anyone how hard it is to cut a parent out of your life. I lost count of how many times I tried to stop talking to my mother," Liz says jokingly.

"I'm glad you didn't," I say with a smile.

"Oh, she loves reminding me every chance she gets that she saved my life." Lizzy laughs, her head dipping slightly, and when the light hits her eyes, it brings back a memory of her from college. She looks even more beautiful now than she did then. "But, that being said, she and I have actually reached a pretty good place in our relationship lately."

"Okay, now I'm the one who can't believe their ears."

"No, really, I mean it." She shoves my arm playfully, and the touch of her skin against mine causes a shiver to travel down my spine. The way she's looking at me, I wonder if she notices my reaction. "Mom is definitely much more tolerable."

"That's great," I offer with a smile. "You look happy."

"I am. Happier than I've been in a long time." I hate that my urge is to ask her if she is dating someone. That's not a question I get to ask anymore. I ruined my chance at a life with Lizzy. She deserves better.

I notice she's staring at me.

"What?" I ask.

"Huh?" she grunts.

"You clearly want to say something," I press.

She bunches her lips into a tight twist before she says, "Do you remember what you told me in college about what you would do career-wise if it wasn't for your father?"

I grin. "I do, but I can't believe you remember."

"How could I forget? You would geek out anytime you talked about how much you loved building furniture."

"Can you imagine me building furniture?" I force a laugh at the ridiculousness of the idea.

"Umm, yes," she says with so much excitement my stomach flutters in response. "You'd be amazing at it. The bassinet you built for Matthew was nothing short of genius."

I don't remember a time when she could say his name without breaking down into tears. She says it now with a smile. She's changed. She's stronger, and she doesn't need me. It's clear she doesn't need anyone, and I couldn't be more proud of her.

"Well, thank you, but genius might be a little generous."

"No. I bet I could find you five customers in an instant. Hell, I'll be your first."

"Oh yeah, in need of some furniture?"

"Actually, yes, I'm moving into my own place next week, and I could use a dining room table."

"By yourself?" I regret asking the question as soon as it leaves my mouth. It's none of my business.

"Me and my guard dog, Cujo."

"Really?"

"No, not really." She laughs. "You became more gullible. Of course, I'm moving out on my own. It's time. I think I overstayed my welcome ever since the wedding."

"That's right!" I'm not surprised I wasn't invited. "How's Emily doing with her marital bliss?"

"They're adorable, of course." She sticks her tongue out and a finger down her throat while making a puke sound for a moment. "I feel like they need their space as a family, though."

"You know I'm only a phone call away if you ever need anything," I tell her.

She bites her bottom lip apprehensively. "I thought after I didn't hear from you for so long that you—" She looks at her drink and takes another sip. "Never mind, it's nothing."

"I'm sorry about that," I say. "I had a lot of guilt to work through."

"Guilt? For what?"

"Come on, Lizzy. I was a pretty terrible husband."

"I mean, I doubt you'll be winning any awards for the husband of the year."

"That's putting it mildly. You needed me, and I turned my back on you."

"Patty was an excellent liar, Nathan. You can't blame yourself for that. Hell, she conned me into signing the divorce papers."

I shake my head. I never imagined she would forgive

me so quickly for my role in ruining her life. I'm not deserving of it, but I am thankful.

"I suppose." I grimace, looking around the coffee shop at all the other faces.

"Do you ever look around at people now and wonder what secrets they're hiding?" Liz asks.

I nod. "All the time. I thought I was the only one."

When I say the words, she instinctively raises a hand to the scar on her face. I reach out slowly, careful not to startle her as I do, hovering over the spot and waiting for her permission. She gives it with a silent nod, and I trace the mark with the backs of my fingers. I see her lip quiver when I do this.

"I think it's beautiful," I say. "Like you."

Her throat moves as she swallows audibly. "Do you think if Matthew hadn't died, things would have happened differently?"

Her question surprises me. Is this what she thinks about? Does she think about the two of us and what could have been? I think about it a lot.

"I believe we were lucky to even have Matthew for a matter of hours. I also think if I hadn't been such an idiot in our marriage, things would have turned out differently."

She jumps, looking at her phone as a timer goes off on it. She silences it and looks up at me.

"Everything okay?" I ask.

"Yeah, that's just my timer letting me know I need to head to work soon." I'm sad when I hear our time has ended so quickly.

"Oh, well, I don't want to keep you if you have some-where to be."

She stands and says, "I probably should go." She hesi-tates. "You know I meant that about needing a dining table."

"I'll see what I can do," I reply, standing as well.

She smiles one last time before she turns in the direc-tion of the door.

"Lizzy," I say her name without thinking, and she spins around to look at me.

"Yes?"

"I enjoyed talking to you."

"Me too."

"Um. Is there any chance you might want to do this again?" Fear flows through me as soon as I ask her the question. I'm not sure I can handle it if she says no. I didn't realize how much I missed her until I saw her.

She steps closer and places her hand on my arm again. "I'd like that."

Instinctively, I wrap my arms around her in an embrace, all the pain we've both been through welling up in the pit of my stomach.

"I know," she whispers, holding me tight in return. "It's so hard."

I nod, and we stand there a few moments longer in the embrace before going our separate ways.

EPILOGUE

FIVE YEARS LATER

"Nathan, we got another letter," Lizzy calls from the living room.

I set my pencil onto the sketches and move into the living room to greet her. "Is it from the Turners?" I ask, eyes wide.

She nods as she tears open the envelope.

"So, how is the superstar enjoying kindergarten?" I ask when we both turn our heads toward the commotion from down the hall. She hands me the letter before walking past me.

"I've got it," she says.

I continue opening the envelope, reading over the greetings and smiling when I see the drawing tucked inside. "They included some of her art," I call out.

"We'll have to add it to the gallery wall," Lizzy replies as she enters the room with Cooper on her hip. He clings onto her as if she were the entire world in his hands.

"Sounds like Madison made some new friends at school," I say.

"Can you imagine what it will be like when Cooper is old enough to start kindergarten?"

"Whoa, can he turn two before we start talking about school?" I tease before I continue reading the letter out loud.

"Madison can't wait until she gets to see Cooper again. She called him her honorary brother to her classmates. They all asked what that meant, and she said he's her brother through her bonus family."

"Oh, Nathan," Lizzy says softly. "I love it."

"I know," I say as I attempt to compose myself. "We should plan a trip back to the city. I miss her."

"Me too," Lizzy replies.

"You know, it's been hard, but I'm glad after her grandmother decided she couldn't raise her either, she was adopted by such an amazing family," I say, staring at the drawing in my hands.

"I still think they should have at least allowed you to be considered for the adoption," Liz mutters as she bounces Cooper on her hip.

"You know that would have been too hard on her. At least her new family is willing to let us be some small part of her life." I walk over and tickle Cooper on his side. He squirms wildly. "And besides, applying for her adoption is what led to this little guy finding his way into our lives."

Lizzy squeezes Cooper into a tighter embrace before setting him down in front of his building blocks. She takes her place next to me, and I wrap an arm around her. "Did you ever think five years ago you would be here?" she asks.

I laugh softly. She isn't wrong at the absurdity of where we are now versus five years ago. After our coffee date, Lizzy asked if I'd consider coming with her to one of her therapy sessions. She was working through the trauma, and her therapist thought it would be good for us to explore some of the things that occurred in our marriage. I almost didn't go. It was around the time Madison's grandmother decided she couldn't be her legal guardian, and I applied to adopt Madison again. I was worried being entangled with Lizzy would hurt my chances.

"I'm so glad you reached out to me," I say, looking at her as she watches Cooper.

"It wasn't a fast road, was it?"

"No, but we're better people for taking it slow," I say.

Last year, soon after we adopted Cooper from the agency that had placed Madison with the Turners, we moved to a small town up north in Maine. Lizzy's mom visits regularly, and Lizzy has even developed a relationship with her sister, though it's certainly a work in progress. Emily and her husband spend weekends up here with us as much as they can. Liz does freelance journalist work while enjoying being a mom, and I'm going after my dream of designing and building furniture.

"Do you ever miss it?" Lizzy asks me.

"Miss what?"

"Your life in Boston?"

"Never."

The End

THE DAY WE DIED

COMING JUNE 22, 2022

PRE-ORDER HERE

Almost two decades after Sydney's father was imprisoned for being the 'Lipstick Killer,' she and her family are finally happy.

They have new identities, and the secret that her father was a notorious serial killer is one Sydney and her mother will never share, not even with her brother, who was an infant when their lives were changed forever.

Sydney has a job she loves processing crime scenes. After several months of dating, she's starting to think she has found a man that could be the one. Just when she starts to allow herself to think her past might actually be behind her, a woman is discovered murdered, wearing the shade of lipstick her father put on the victims of his brutal killings.

As more evidence turns up, Sydney must decide if she should go to the police and risk blowing up this new life they've built or keep quiet?

NEWSLETTER

Do you want to make sure you don't miss any upcoming releases or giveaways? Be sure to sign up for my newsletter at http://signup.wendyowensbooks.com/

ACKNOWLEDGMENTS

To my readers: I wouldn't be able to do what I do without your desire to read my books. Thank you from the bottom of my heart. In addition to readers there is an army of bloggers, ARC readers, and book tokkers that read and review my books. Your time is deeply appreciated and I am honored you have taken your time to read and review my work. Thank you.

Thank you to all the editors who worked on this book. My grammar is terrible and without you I would look like an idiot.

A deep and endless thank you to Kiki, Colleen, and everyone at The Next Step PR. You have helped my books find their way into the hands of so many new readers this year and without your help I would not be able to do what I love to do.

Zoe, Brayden, and Penelope, you all make me proud every single day and you have made me a better human. Thank you for being my motivation to get up and keep going every day.

Thank you to the love of my life, Josh. I don't deserve the deepness of your love, but I'm so happy you disagree. Thank you for supporting my dreams.

ABOUT THE AUTHOR

Wendy Owens, was raised in the small college town of Oxford, Ohio. She happily spends her days writing—her three dogs curled up at her feet. When she's not writing, Wendy can be found spending time with her true love, her tech geek husband, Josh, and their three amazing kids. As a hobby Wendy enjoys drawing and painting.

To follow everything current with Wendy Owens' Books:
https://signup.wendyowensbooks.com/

Made in the USA
Coppell, TX
21 December 2023

26708980R00144